CALLED BY A DRAGON

CHRISTINE BORN

Present Day Avalanya

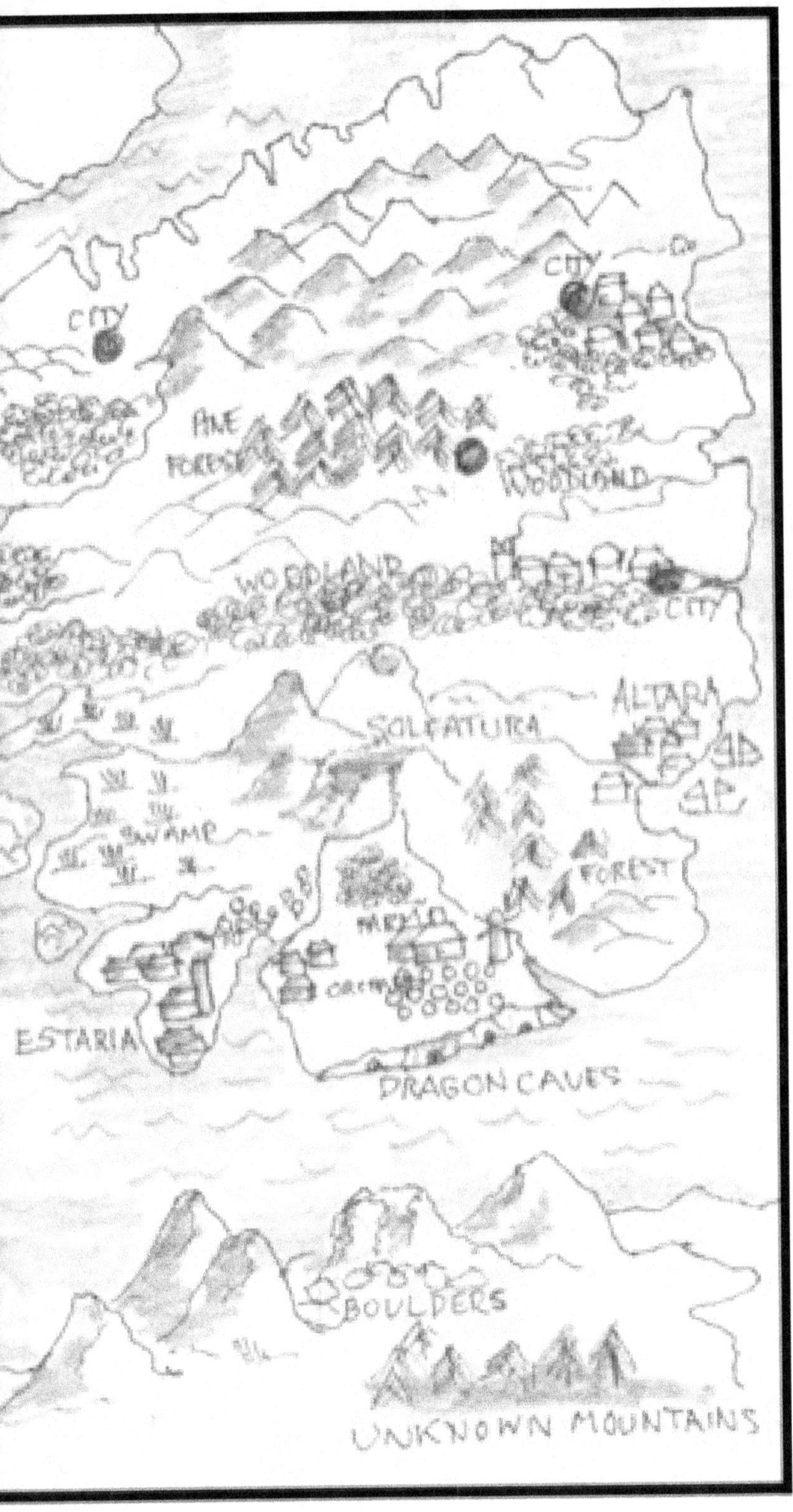

CITY
CITY
PINE FOREST
WOODLAND
WOODLAND
CITY
SOLFATURA
ALTARA
FOREST
SWAMP
FIELD
CAVE
ESTARIA
DRAGON CAVES
BOULDERS
UNKNOWN MOUNTAINS

CALLED BY A DRAGON
Williamsburg, Virginia

Copyright 2023 Christine Born
ISBN 979-8-9891979-0-3
ISBN 979-8-9891979-1-0 (epub)

Although this is a work of fiction, it is set in a real place in England. The Jurassic Coast is a prehistoric wonder and is the only UNESCO World Heritage site in Britain. It's easily accessible, and anyone can walk on the beaches and find fossils, such as ammonites. Many of the places mentioned in the story are real, but the holiday cottage is fictional, as is the woodland behind it.

DEDICATION

To my grandchildren.

CHAPTER ONE

"I'M GOING TO LOOK for a dinosaur as soon as we get there!" said Will from the back of the car.

"Don't be silly They're extinct," said Nat. "It's the Jurassic coast; not the movie *Jurassic Park*! I think you're getting mixed up."

"I know that. I meant I'm going to look for fossils. My books say lots of them have been found where we're going." Although Will was only ten—two years younger than his twin brothers, Nat and Pete —he did a lot of research when he was interested in something.

"It might be hard to find any because so many people have already found a lot of the really big stuff, haven't they, Mum?" continued Nat. "You studied geology. Did you ever come down here and look for fossils?"

"I tried looking once, but I found mostly ammonites. We can certainly search for those. The house we're renting for our summer vacation is a short walk from the beach."

"Sounds cool, doesn't it, Pete? Pete? Hey! Are you listening? You've been really quiet since we left home," Nat said to his brother sitting in the front seat.

Pete, jolted from his daydream, sat up suddenly. His short, dark hair stood up in spikes as if he had been electrocuted. So different from Nat's long ponytail, his hairstyle only emphasized that the twins looked nothing alike.

"Sorry. I was miles away. There's something bugging me. I don't know what it is, but it's annoying."

"Are you okay?" asked their mother. "I do hope you aren't getting sick just as we begin the holiday. Do you want me to stop the car so we could walk around a bit?"

"No thanks. I'll be all right. If we aren't too far away, I'd rather keep going. Can you tell us more about where we're staying?"

"The house is a small, three-bed cottage dating from the sixteenth century. There's one big bedroom where Dad and I will sleep when he's here. One of the other bedrooms has bunk beds. Pete and Nat, you will have those, and Will can have the smaller room. There's a small front garden opening straight onto the road, and a larger one at the back leading up the hillside to some woodland."

"We'll be able to do lots of climbing, I hope," put in Nat.

"You won't be able to do much because the cliffs around there are dangerous. In fact, that's how many of the fossils were found. When parts of the cliff fall away, they expose more layers. Be very careful not to get too close to the cliffs. You'll have to restrict your climbing activities to scrambling over rocks on the beach."

"We'll find things to do." Then he was struck by another thought. "There is Wi-Fi, isn't there?"

"Yes. That was something I made sure of, but we're here for lots of fresh air and exercise, so there won't be time for sitting around playing on your electronic devices. I want you all to get out as much as possible. Including you, Pete. No burying your head in a book all day."

"I'm not so sure about this. First, I can't climb, and now I can't play video games. What do you think, Pete?"

"It's no use talking to him anymore," said Will. "He's daydreaming again by the look of it."

"I might as well stop talking to you if you never listen to me." Nat thumped Pete on the back of the head.

"Ow! Are we nearly there?"

Nat pointed down the road. "Does our cottage have a thatched roof? Because the GPS says we're close."

"That does look like ours," said their mum.

There was no garage but plenty of space to park the car when they pulled in front of the cottage. After Mum parked, they jumped out and waited eagerly for her to unlock the door which opened into a tiny hallway.

Once inside, they ran into the first room on the left. "Hey, there's a nice big TV and a fireplace if it gets cold," Will pointed out.

"Never mind that now. We've got the whole place to explore first." Nat tore off down the hall past stairs on the right. The boys rushed after him into what was a surprisingly large kitchen. A long wooden table with a bench on one side and four wooden chairs opposite with more chairs at either end stood ready at one end of the room.

"I'm absolutely starving," said Nat.

"The food and snacks are still in the car. We need to unpack first," their mother said.

Nat pointed at the countertop. "Look at that! It's a cake and there's a note."

WELCOME TO SUNNYSIDE COTTAGE. HERE'S A SPECIALITY OF THE AREA CALLED DORSET APPLE CAKE THAT YOU CAN ENJOY AS YOU BEGIN WHAT WE HOPE WILL BE A VERY PLEASANT STAY.

"Now that's what I call hospitality. It looks like you get your wish after all and can eat before unpacking. I'll put a kettle on. Hey, where are you off to now?" Mum asked.

"I'm gonna see what's upstairs while the kettle's heating," said Nat. His brothers chased after him, taking the narrow stairs two at a time.

Two bunkbeds stood sentinel in the first room. "Wow,

that's cool. Look at those beams with rope tied around them on the ceiling," said Nat.

"I know what they're for," said Will. "I've seen it in books; it's to tie the thatch on from the outside."

Nat climbed the ladder to the bunk to have a closer look. "First dibs on the top bunk."

Will left them to argue about who should sleep in the top bunk. He yelled from his room, "Mine has a view of the sea. I'd rather sleep on my own anyway and not listen to you two carrying on."

"Boys! Boys! I thought you were hungry. Come down before I eat all this cake myself!" called their mother.

Almost falling down the stairs, they ran back to the kitchen to grab a plate and a mug of tea each.

"Yummy cake." Nat stuffed a huge slice in his mouth.

"You certainly gobbled that down fast, but don't run away. You still have to clear our stuff out of the car," said their mother. "And put it away neatly!"

With everyone helping, it was soon done. They didn't have to make up the beds which were all ready for them.

"This place is so old, it could even be haunted. Maybe that's why Pete was feeling so funny, Will. The ghosts were calling him, OOH OOOH," Nat moaned.

"You're trying to scare me. I'm going to tell Mum," said Will.

Pete ignored them, making his way to the back door.

"Hey, Pete, stop! What do you want to go out that way for?" asked Nat. "That isn't the way to the beach. Aren't you interested in exploring down there first? There's plenty of time to see the back. I vote we go see the beach first. Will agrees with me, don't you? Don't you?"

Will said, "Come on, Pete. We've been cooped up in the car for hours. I want to run around some."

Pete hesitated but said firmly, "No. I've got to see those woods first, but if you won't come with me, I'm going by myself." He made toward the door again.

"What on earth is the matter with you today? You aren't acting normally. You're behaving like a zombie without a mind of your own. This place must really be haunted, but it's only affecting you. We're fine.

"I can't help it," said Pete. "I feel strange. It's like I'm in a dream. There's something in my head, and it feels like my brain is going round and round. I don't understand it. I can't go anywhere but up there."

"No, we're going down to the beach. Aren't we, Will?"

But before Will could agree, Pete opened the back door and started up the hill.

Nat chased after him, grabbing him by the arm. "Don't be a spoilsport. We came here to be by the sea, not some old trees we can see anywhere."

Pete struggled to get away, shouting in a foreign language and hitting out wildly at Nat, who promptly kicked back.

Their mother rushed to separate them. "What's going on? We haven't been here five minutes, and you're already fighting. What's up with you?"

"It's Pete's fault. He started it. He won't come down to the beach with us!" said Will.

"I can't go down there. I can't say why. I've just got to! I feel so bad; I think I'm going to throw up any minute."

Their mother anxiously looked him up and down. "Oh my goodness me, what's the matter? You look dreadful. You're white as a sheet. I think we'd better go inside."

Once they had dragged a protesting Pete indoors, he collapsed onto the sofa, curling up into a ball and hugging himself. "It's awful; I feel so miserable."

Looking closely at him and feeling his forehead, his mother saw tears welling up in his eyes. "Oh dear, I'm not sure what to do. You don't have a fever. It could be that you overdid things studying for your exams before we left. You always did get anxious before an exam. Nat, can you get him a warm drink please? And maybe find some crackers."

"No, I want fish," Pete said.

"B-b-but you don't even like fish very much," said Nat.

"Well, we are at the seaside so maybe we could find some fish and chips close by," their mother said.

"No, don't do that," said Pete in a normal voice again. "Don't know why I said that. I'm so mixed up in my brain."

"Look, Mum! He's almost back to his normal color now." Nat plopped down on the couch next to Pete.

"You're right. He does look better. Why don't you and Will look around the beach while I see about getting us all some supper? Then maybe he'll feel better. But don't be too long or I'll worry about you as well!"

"Sorry, Mum. I felt horrible, but it's not so bad now. You're right. I was studying hard at school. I never found exams easy. I'll help you with the meal. Nat, if you pass those tourist shops buy me some chocolate. That will help me to feel even better."

"You got better in a hurry. Are you sure you weren't making it up?" said Nat.

"That's enough teasing. Go on out before I change my mind," said their mother.

As soon as they were gone, Pete said. "What are you going to fix? Can we have pasta?"

"Yes, we can. Nat was right; you did recover quickly. Make yourself useful and put water on to boil."

By the time the other two returned, the meal was ready, and everyone devoured it as fast as they could.

"Did you bring me chocolate?" asked Pete.

"If they did, it will have to wait until you've cleared the dishes. You may be on vacation, but you still have chores to do."

With the work done, they settled down to eat the chocolate and talk about the beach.

"It looks fun. There's a cove like a giant horseshoe and a pebbly beach. No sand though," said Will.

They talked excitedly, looking through leaflets about the area.

"You're finally tired," said their mother when Will yawned. "Time to get ready for bed. I'm a bit tired myself after that long drive."

"I'm too excited to sleep," said Nat, but he didn't argue when they went up to get ready for bed.

Even with all the excitement, Nat and Will fell soundly asleep as soon as their heads hit the pillows.

Not so for Pete. He heard a voice in his head again and tossed and turned for ages. When he finally did fall asleep, he dreamed vividly. He was on a blue dragon . . .

No sooner had he looked around and seen the palest of green skies, then he was being dragged down into a deep dark green ocean and couldn't breathe. Frightened out of his wits, he thought he was about to drown when a calm voice in his mind told him to relax. He found he could breathe normally but with streams of bubbles coming out of his mouth.

This must be what it is like to be a fish, he thought.

When he stopped struggling, he found himself surrounded by dolphins. He had recovered from his panic and was playing when the dream changed.

Something squeezed him, tightly wrapped around his body. He began to panic again.

I don't like this. I must wake up. But he couldn't seem to. He kicked and screamed. The more he tried to get out of what was enveloping him, the tighter it got.

Help me! he screamed while trying to break free.

Suddenly, whatever was holding him burst apart, and as his eyes unstuck, a bright light hit him in the face.

A ray of sunlight shone from a window next to his bed. His bedsheets were tangled around him. *What next?*

Scrambling out of the tangle, he stared at the ceiling, trying to recall details from the dreams. They receded as dreams often do. Unable to remember all the details from the jumble in his mind, he sat up slowly, listening for Nat, but he continued to snore.

Wide awake, Pete dressed and went downstairs in search of something to eat. He was surprised to see his mother already up and drinking tea.

"How come you're awake so early?" asked Pete.

"Well, you may laugh, but the gulls woke me up. It's such an unusual sound to hear, and I forgot we're at the seaside. Not that I mind. It's better than cars going by and garbagemen emptying bins. You look a lot better. What woke you up?"

"Actually, I had a rough night's sleep."

"What disturbed you?"

"I had awful nightmares."

"What were they about?"

"I don't remember clearly, and I'd rather forget them. It probably has to do with this stuff going on in my head. And, before you ask, I haven't been bothered too much this morning." *But I still need to go up that hill!*

"Why don't you help me with breakfast?"

They busied themselves cooking eggs, toast, sausages, and bacon. No sooner had they finished, then the other two appeared.

"Now that's what I call a scrumptious breakfast!" exclaimed Nat when they had finished. "Thanks a lot, Mum. As soon as we've cleared the dishes, why don't we go to the beach? And then we'll go with Pete up the hill."

"I thought we'd go up there this morning. If you won't come with me, I'll go on my own." Pete crossed his arms over his chest. He wasn't going to be deterred this time.

Their mother, sensing another argument brewing, stepped in. "Why don't you put a few snacks and drinks in a backpack and go exploring? There are maps on the bookshelf in the sitting room, and on our drive down the hill, I noticed several footpath signs. If you start behind the cottage, you might find a shortcut to the closest one. That way Pete can get his wish, and you can probably circle back down into the village. Besides, you can get a good view from up there and see where you want to go first."

"Okay. At least if we go that way, Pete will be satisfied." Nat took his plates to the sink.

"I'll make a deal with you. If we don't find anything strange up there, I will try my utmost to put it out of my mind, and I promise I won't mention it ever again. I can't say fairer than that, can I?"

After packing snacks, Nat and Will marched up the hillside to the woods following Pete. The back garden was quite large with a shed at the top. Opening its door to look inside, they discovered folding chairs, a small picnic table, water and sand toys, a large beach umbrella, fishing nets, and even an old lobster pot hanging on hooks on the wall.

Nat noticed a coil of thick rope. "That could be useful if there's any climbing to do."

"You better not forget what Mum said about the cliffs being dangerous around here," warned Pete. "I don't think we need to take it with us."

Leaving the garden, they looked at the village below. "It's so peaceful. In fact, the whole place is quiet except for the sound of the sea and gulls. Doesn't seem as though anything exciting could ever happen here, does it?" Nat threw a rock down the hill.

"Look at that dark wood in front of us," said Will. "With those moss-covered rocks and ivy, it looks gloomy."

Nat peered into the woods. "The tree cover is so thick, there's hardly any sunlight getting through them."

Pete suddenly stopped and stood motionless with a vacant look on his face.

"Oh no, not again. What's up this time?" Nat asked him, but Pete just stood there.

"You know, I don't think he hears us. What's going on with him?" Will asked.

They shouted at Pete, and Nat grabbed his arm and shook him. "I don't like this very much. Maybe there's something seriously wrong, and we should go back right now."

"No, I'm okay." Pete shook his head. "It's just . . . I'm hearing these sounds in my head. Almost like jumbled up words, and they aren't making any sense. I think it's coming from over there." He pointed toward a group of particularly large rocks, then took off for them.

It was hard to make out details in the dim light. Without any warning, he stopped again. "That's so weird. Between those two large boulders, there's an opening, and the vines are waving like they're being blown by a wind, but there isn't any breeze. Do you see it?"

"I don't see anything," Nat said.

"Those vines aren't moving," Will added.

Pete pushed some of the creepers aside and leaned forward, holding onto the sides of the rock. "There's an opening behind this ivy with a little light coming from somewhere inside, but it's too dark to see anything clearly."

He edged slowly and carefully forward. Suddenly, with a sharp cry of surprise, Pete fell.

"Ouch!" Pete yelled, then all was quiet.

Nat and Will rushed forward to where they had last seen him. Feeling around anxiously, they found the opening Pete had mentioned, but there was no sign of him. Only a dark tunnel sloping down steeply in between a lot of creepers and vines. A faint light glowed from somewhere.

"What happened?" Nat called to him. "Are you all right?"

When there was no answer, Nat said to Will, "I'm going down to see what happened. He must be hurt. Remember that rope we saw in the shed? Run and get it in case this tunnel is too steep and we have to carry him back up."

As Will rushed off, Nat called out again. "Pete, are you okay?"

Pete shouted back, "Yes, I'm okay, but something very strange is going on. Do you have your phone with you? I dropped mine when I fell. Switch on the torch. "

Nat quickly found his, but it only glowed faintly down the tunnel, barely illuminating the sides and pieces of rock sticking out here and there. "I can climb down to reach you."

"Be careful. It's slippery!"

"No wonder you fell. I think I can use the vines to hold onto." Nat slowly lowered himself into the opening.

When he reached the bottom, Nat shone his light over Pete, examining him for injuries. "What happened?"

"I started sliding. I tried to grab the vines, but I couldn't stop myself. Luckily, I landed on something soft, but I hit my head on something hard." Pete rubbed the back of his head.

"Are you bleeding?" He flashed the light on the back of Pete's head.

"No, but I burned my hand." He held his hand up to the light where there was a tiny mark.

"On what? There's nothing down here."

"I touched something when I tried to get up, and I heard gibberish words."

They looked around.

"This is seriously weird, Pete. Perhaps you banged your head harder than you thought."

Suddenly Pete yelled, "Get me out of here! I cannot breathe! Get me out of here! NOW!"

Pete fell to the ground in a tight ball, clasping his hands over his head. A new voice sounded from his mouth. "Oh no! Do not go away after I worked so hard to get you here. Please listen to me and help me. I am so squashed, and it is getting worse. I have been here so long, and it is so hard on my own. When are you going to listen to me properly?"

Pete kicked and punched, narrowly missing Nat who reached out to touch him. Nat punched Pete in the arm.

"What did you do that for?" Pete's voice was back to normal as he rubbed his arm.

Nat looked wildly around the cave. "We have to get out of here. I think you're feeling shut in. I think some people get it when they're in a small space. And you were shouting something; it didn't sound like your voice." He pointed at a sliver of light. "That light might be a way out. We can't risk the climb back up in your state. Come with me."

"I don't want to go! I have to stay here! It wants me!" Half dragging him, Nat made his way toward the light, but large rocks blocked the way. He pushed and pushed at them, but they wouldn't move. "It's no use. We'd better go back. We'd need dynamite to shift this."

All of a sudden, there was a grinding sound, and a large boulder moved with a jerk, dislodging more rocks as it went.

Blinded by the brightness in front of them, Pete and Nat were unable to see anything at first. Shading their eyes, they stared out the opening over a the pile of debris. Amazed and shocked into silence, they gazed in wonder at the incredible scene before them.

CHAPTER TWO

EMERALD GREEN WAVES TOPPED with soft white foam gently lapped against a beach of golden sand. A faintly briny smell wafted in the air, and the horizon was completely clear of ships. Only a few unusual birds resembling gulls soared and squawked in a pale-green sky. Silver fish with glittering scales sparkled in the ocean. Farther out at sea, a snowcapped, mountainous landmass gleamed in the sun.

Clutching at his brother in awe, Nat finally found his voice and whispered, "Please tell me I'm dreaming. This is unbelievable."

But Pete wasn't listening. He pushed Nat's hands away. "I need to get back inside the cave. Something wants me to go back into that cave."

"Stop going on about that stupid cave and look around you. This is *not* the cove where our cottage is. This is not where we came from!"

Calming down, Pete looked around. "You're right. We weren't this close to the sea when we started up that hill. Where are we?"

Nat pointed. "Look! Someone's coming around those cliffs at the end of the beach."

They watched as a girl about their age ran toward them, coming to a stop in front of them.

Her long, black ponytail swayed back and forth as she looked between the brothers with her bright green eyes.

"Hi," Nat said when the silence grew too long.

The girl continued to stare.

Nat studied her. He noticed the light orange tunic top belted around her waist, short-sleeved white shirt, and loose dark blue pants rolled up to her knees. "That's not modern dress," he whispered to Pete. "And I've never seen anyone with eyes that color."

"Hallo." Nat held out his hand.

She jumped back and dropped the bag she had been carrying over her shoulder.

Then shyly she said, "*Yăvăvoyā.*"

"Sounds like a foreign language. Maybe it's Chinese? I only know a few words." Pete scratched his head.

"*Devŏ'oya vocanaã,*" she said.

Nat and Pete tried out as many foreign words as they could come up with, but she only shook her head.

She pointed to herself. "*Bre'chettyă.*"

"*Bre'kettyaah,*" repeated Pete, pointing at her.

She smiled and nodded.

Encouraged by this, he pointed to himself. "Pete."

"Peeta," she imitated.

She pointed to his brother, and Pete said, "Nat."

"Nat." She tested the word on her tongue and giggled.

She pointed to different things around them, followed by more of her language. They managed to get *she'ăh*, which might have been her word for sea. She held her hand out to the beach and said *shăĝa*, which they thought might mean sand. A few other sounds they were unable to pronounce.

"This is certainly going to be slow going if this is all we can do." Nat shook his head in frustration. "At this rate, we'll never find out where we are."

The girl clapped her hands as though an idea had struck her. Picking up a piece of driftwood, she drew stick figures in the sand. They touched each other's heads with their hands. Then she drew speech bubbles with funny writing within them. Putting her fingers to her own temples then pointing to Pete's head, she mimed putting her hands to his head and vice versa.

"What do you think, Nat? Should I try it?"

"We're getting nowhere fast, so give it a go, but I'd rather it was you than me."

"I don't see how it could hurt."

Very gingerly, Pete moved closer to the girl and nodded his consent. She took his hands and placed one on each side of her head, put her hands on his head, and closed her eyes. Almost immediately, he felt a warm pressure and incoherent sounds tumbling around in his brain. A little scared, he prepared to shove her away when words came into his head. He almost jumped out of his skin.

Do not worry or be frightened. I am trying to meld with your thought waves so I can imprint my language on you. You will be able to understand and speak our language, although we will not be able to understand yours. Do not move; it is not yet completed.

"It's all right," she said after a few seconds, dropping her hands and removing his. "Now we can talk properly."

He looked at the girl in surprise. "Wow! I can understand you now.

"What's going on? What are you saying? I can't understand you!" Nat's voice rose in panic.

"What did he say, Pete?" asked the girl.

"Can't you hear him? He says he can't understand me now. What did you do to me?"

"Oh! Of course! I can only do one mind meld, so when you are talking to me, he can't understand you. He will only understand you if you are looking directly at him. What we need is someone else to meld with him."

She closed her eyes and stood very still for a few seconds.

When she opened them, she said, "I have just called my sister Izzy and asked her to join us to mind meld with your friend."

Pete turned to his brother and repeated what Brecky had told him.

"Thank goodness you're speaking English again. I thought I was cracking up," Nat said.

Brecky touched Pete's arm. "While we're waiting, tell me your name again."

"I'm Pete and this is my twin brother Nat."

Brecky looked at Nat's long, fair ponytail and freckles. "He doesn't look like you."

Pete shrugged. "Not all twins look alike. What did you say your name was?"

"Call me Brecky. It's easier." She looked down the beach. "Here comes Izzy."

Izzy was dressed in a similar fashion to Brecky, wearing a blue tunic top and brown pants. Her hair was shorter, but she, too, had large, unusual eyes that shone yellow-green.

"Hi, Brecky, What's up?"

Brecky gestured toward Pete. "This is Pete and his twin brother Nat. I don't know where they came from, but they don't speak our language. I did a mind meld with Pete, but now Nat needs a mind meld too. Can you do one with him?"

Pete turned to face Nat. "Brecky just asked her sister to do a mind meld with you. Copy what you saw me do with Brecky."

When Izzy had completed the meld, Nat exclaimed, "Wow! How do you and Brecky do this?"

"Our mother taught us. She's one of a few born with the ability. It often runs in families. She taught me when we met a group of people who came from the south. They didn't speak our language either. Luckily the meld lasts forever, and once done, you'll be able to speak and understand any Avalanyan. I can only meld with one person at a time. That's why I called Izzy here."

"Is Pete the one who has been calling you?" Izzy asked Brecky.

Pete shook his head. "I didn't even know you existed."

"But Pete's been hearing strange things too. I think they're coming from that cave." Nat shuddered. "Pete was acting weirder than usual and talking in a bizarre voice."

"I did? I don't remember."

"You were asking me not to go away. You said you were squashed and had been in the cave a long time. That was dumb. We hadn't been in there that long. We were waiting for Will to come back with the rope."

"Oh no! I forgot all about Will! I hope he won't try to climb down by himself. We shouldn't have left him so long," Pete said.

"Who is Will?" Brecky asked.

"He's our younger brother. We have to go back for him."

Nat put a hand on Pete's shoulder. "Why don't you stay here while I go back inside the cave to get Will? I don't need you freaking out on me again."

Nat climbed quickly back up the rockfall into the cave, leaving his brother with the two girls.

Help me!

Pete flinched as the voice yelled inside his head.

Brecky's eyes were wide when she turned to him. "Did you hear that? There's someone in trouble near here."

"You heard that voice?"

"A voice called me to this part of the beach, and then I saw you. Izzy thought I was making up the voices in my head."

"It did sound a little crazy," Izzy said. "Pete, if Nat's gone for your brother, we'll need our sister Lanya to do another mind meld. I'll call her." She closed her eyes.

In no time, another girl joined them.

"What's up, Brecky?" Lanya asked.

Brecky tugged her over to meet her new friend. "Lanya, meet Pete. He and his brother Nat just came out of that cave over there." She pointed at it. "I don't understand exactly where they're from. There's another brother called Will still in the cave, and Nat went to get him. They speak a different language from us. Izzy and I did the meld with Pete and Nat, but we'll need you to meld with the other boy.

~~~~~

When Nat entered the cave, he was surprised to see that it was much brighter. A glow lit up the cave. He peered up at the opening above. "Will, are you there?"

"I'm here. Is Pete okay?"

"He's fine. I'm sorry we disappeared on you. You'll never believe what's been happening. Did you get the rope?"

"I just got back."

"What took you so long?"

"I ran as fast as I could. You couldn't have been quicker."

"I don't understand. We've been gone for ages," Nat mumbled under his breath. He yelled back up to his brother, "Can you tie the rope to a tree trunk or something? Then hold onto it and come on down. You'll see rocks jutting out to put your feet on as you go but take it easy."

Will quickly scampered down the rocks and headed for the shining oval. "What's that?"

"Don't touch it. Follow me quickly. I'll tell you later."

Will followed him out of the cave and stopped short when he caught his first glimpse of the emerald-green sea and the lime green sky.

"What trick are you pulling now? This is seriously unreal."

"Hi, Will," said Pete. "Welcome to Avalanya! This is Brecky, Izzy, and Lanya. They live here."

"*Yăvăvoyā*," the sisters said in unison.

"This is another of your stupid games, and I won't play it!" Will stamped his foot.

"We're not messing with you, Will," said Nat. "When we got here, we couldn't understand what they were saying either.
~~~~~

Luckily, they can teach their language to us through some kind of magic trick."

Pete took up the explanation. "They have this thing called a mind meld where they exchange thoughts with you. Nat and I both did it, and it's quite fantastic. This is Lanya. All you have to do is touch each other's heads. When you do that, presto! You get to speak and understand her language."

"That's crazy." Will folded his arms and turned his back on Pete and Nat.

"Brecky, Will doesn't believe us. He won't do the mind meld. Do you think we could show him what we did?" Pete asked. Looking at his brother, he said, "Come on, Will, watch us."

Brecky and Pete touched each other's head to show Will what he would have to do.

Will shook his head even harder. "I've had enough. I'm going home."

Nat pleaded with him. "Please trust us. It's as Pete said. We really don't understand where we are, how we got here, or even what this place is. All we know is that these girls can use some kind of magic to get their language inside our brains. It's like some kind of mind transfer. Some trick, eh? You've got to do it too, or we'll never get any further with this mystery."

"You'll feel a weird sensation like a kind of tingling, and then all these foreign words come tumbling into your brain. It's like being in a science fiction movie," Pete said.

"No way!" shrieked Will. "Let a strange girl touch me? You've got to be kidding!"

"Look here," said Pete. "We can't sit here arguing about this all day. I'll let you play my new Xbox if you do this. "

Reluctantly, Will allowed Lanya to place his hands on her head, then she touched his head. He almost jumped out of his skin.

His face mirrored his astonishment as he found himself able to understand Lanya's words.

Everybody started talking at once, until Pete interrupted. "Please, now can we do something about this voice pleading with us from inside the cave? I think it has something to do with that rock I fell on."

Pete filled Will in on the shock he had received when he touched the rock and showed him the mark on his hand.

As a group, they entered the cave. The glowing blue rock was even brighter than before.

Pete and Brecky exchanged a worried look.

"What's wrong?" Nat asked them.

"It's the voice. It's coming from that rock." Pete pointed at the bright light. He waved the others closer. "Did you hear that?"

Everyone else shook their heads, but Brecky exclaimed, "It's not a rock! It's an egg. Or it's in the egg. It wants help getting out."

"Look how big it is! It's larger than an ostrich's egg." Will stared wide-eyed at the smooth surface.

Pete waved the others closer to the egg. "It's been trapped for millions of years so the shell has become too hard. We need to pull at the edges of the crack to help it get out."

"You said it shocked you." Nat held his hands up, palms out.

"Only when I fell on it."

The egg glowed the turquoise of the sea and rocked gently. Lines led from a small crack on the top.

"The voice says we should put our hands here and pull at the edges of this crack," Pete said.

"Are you sure about this?" asked Will. "Something dreadful might come out of it. I'm scared."

Pete snorted a short laugh. "It says not to be such a ninny."

Brecky added, "We needn't be frightened. It won't hurt us. We need to help it."

They gripped the edges of the crack. With a mighty pull, pieces of the shell started to come away.

CHAPTER THREE

TWO LARGE, GOLDEN EYES glittered from a turquoise head. Two horns stood on her head, and long, wet, tendrils hung from her face. A frill-like structure ringed her neck.

A trembling Will grabbed his brothers' hands. The girls flung their arms around each other in breathless fear. Rooted to the ground, they watched the long, sinuous creature struggle to climb out.

"It's a beautiful baby dragon. It even has tiny wings." Brecky let go of her sister and ran to help it. "Ouch! Don't touch the horns. They're sharp."

Her eyes opened wide as she heard a soft musical voice in her head.

Oh, thank you thank you. What a relief to be out!

Pete jumped, letting go of Will's hand. "Did you hear that? Or is it only in my head?"

He rushed to help Brecky with the dragon.

The others shook their heads, holding back.

Please tell your friends to come and meet me. I am not going to hurt any of them, but I am feeling a bit unsteady and want to get outside into the daylight.

"It's not going to hurt you. It even sounds gentle, and it wants us to help it out of the rest of the shell and out of the cave," Pete told them.

Looking a bit nervous, they came forward reluctantly. Will held tightly onto Nat who grasped Izzy and Lanya. Joining Pete and Brecky, they all gingerly helped the little creature out onto the beach.

Peter and Brechettya, get everyone to form a circle around me with their hands on my head. Although I can speak to anyone, this connection will make it easier for us to communicate.

Still wary, they did as Pete said when he told them what the dragon wanted.

Now it is time for the rest of you to join yourselves properly in friendship to me.

Startled, they jumped backward when they heard her soft voice in their heads, but then a feeling of utter joy and happiness came over them. They laughed and cried at the same time. In fact, everyone was so overcome with feelings of friendship and love, they wished the moment would go on forever and ever! The boys exchanged high fives, and the girls put their arms around each other. Lanya and Will were so overwhelmed with delight that they hugged the dragon as well.

A broad grin split Will's face. "That was unbelievable. Seeing and hearing a real dragon!"

They all gazed with wonder at the beautiful, Labrador-sized dragon before them. Several spikes ran down its glistening, snake-like body that was covered in turquoise scales all the way down to its four web-footed claws. Stubby, fin-like wings protruded from its back. Its sides held frilled fins while its long tail ended in an enormous, flat fin, resembling the tailfin of a whale.

Hallo to you all. I am a Water Dragon, and my name is Jessynta. I know Peter and Brecchettya. You are my bond mates. Peter, you bonded to me when you first touched my shell, and when you touched my horn, Brecchettya, so did you.

"This is getting to be a habit, touching everyone we meet. I'm not too sure about going around getting this friendly with everybody in the world." But Will couldn't suppress his grin.

Touching me was only to enable you to hear me. Although I can always hear you.

Pete saw that Will was anxious and gave him a quick hug.

"What do you mean by bond mates? Are we bond mates too?" asked Will.

No, although you are my friends, Peter and Brecchettya have special responsibilities. They are going to help me as I grow.

"Is that why they have marks on their hands?"

Yes, the mark only happens to special bond mates. Now please gather up my shell pieces. They are important.

"You can call me Brecky. Our Avalanyan names are so long, we usually shorten them. Not everyone has a special Avalanyan name like us. It was our mother's idea. She thought it important to carry on the tradition of old Avalanyan names, so they won't be lost."

"We shorten our names too," said Pete.

Names have a very special meaning to dragons, and we always use the full names given to us by our mothers. It is not polite to use a short version.

To everyone's horror, Pete and Brecky suddenly clutched their stomachs as if in pain.

"I'm starving. Is there anything to eat?" said Pete.

Brecky gasped out, "Me too."

Before the others could open their mouths to speak Jessynta said, *It is because you are bonded to me that you can feel my emotions, and I am, in fact, starving. It was quite hard work getting out of that shell. I feel like I will waste away to a skeleton if I do not eat soon. You should have offered me something to eat the moment I got out of my shell.*

Pete was a little surprised by Jessynta's sharp words but recovered quickly. "We've got a few snacks and drinks in our backpacks up by the cave entrance, but I don't imagine they would be enough to feed a dragon."

"I've just been fishing and left nets full of fish on the beach," said Lanya.

As a water dragon, my favorite food is fish. In a few weeks' time, I will be big enough to catch my own food, but right now, I welcome your help.

Lanya left to fetch the fish from the nets.

Izzy said, "I'll get food of our own from just up the beach a little way. We were planning to stay here for a picnic before all this happened."

The others returned to the cave to gather the shell pieces into the sack that Brecky had dropped earlier. Nat picked up the backpacks, and they carried everything to the beach where the dragon waited.

When Lanya returned, the dragon gave a mighty roar and tore into the fish, swallowing them whole while everyone watched in amazement.

The humans sat on the beach and shared their food.

"What are these funny things? They taste salty, but they're good." Lanya licked her fingers.

"We call them crisps. They're thin-sliced, deep-fried potatoes." Pete held up round, yellowish item. "I like this funny fruit, especially this one which looks like a cross between an apple and a banana but tastes fizzy!"

"How is it that the drinks have stayed so cold on this hot day?" said Izzy.

"We have them in this special bag that is frozen," said Nat.

Izzy looked puzzled. "How did you do that?"

Nat tried to explain a refrigerator but found it too difficult.

Will crammed his mouth full. "That bread tastes so yummy, I could easily eat the whole loaf."

Pete licked his lips. "Cheese is my favorite food, but I've never eaten any as good as that."

"We have a farm, and our mother bakes bread every day. We also make our cheese," said Brecky.

Lanya clapped her hands together. "I've just had an idea. Jessynta, could you spare us a few fish you're wolfing down so fast? We could build a fire and cook some."

Certainly, and you do not need to build a fire. I forgot you humans like to cook your food, but I can help. I believe I have eaten enough to produce a small flame, so choose a few fish from my pile and move a little distance away.

They did so and watched with open mouths as she took a deep breath and spouted a flame to barbecue the fish. They picked up the cooked fish and cut it into bite-sized pieces.

"Now that's a super trick," said Will, clapping his hands. "I could get to like this place and our new friends. I usually don't eat fish, but if it always tasted as good as that, I could eat it more often."

When they were full, Nat said, "Can you tell us more about this place? It doesn't look like anywhere I've ever seen before. A beautiful dragon out of a fairy tale. You three here, speaking a language we couldn't understand. That mind meld thing. Your funny clothes. I'm beginning to think I'm dreaming."

"Don't call our clothes funny. Yours are funny to us too," said Brecky. "Everything about you is strange. Unusual anyway." She pointed to their feet.

"They're called trainers or sneakers," Pete said.

Izzy looked closely at his shirt. "What are those strange pictures and the squiggly marks?"

Pete touched his chest. "These are t-shirts. Mine has a badge of my favorite sports team. Nat's wearing one with a picture of his favorite music group, and Will's wearing one from his favorite movie. We have a lot of different T-shirts to choose from."

Will scratched his head. "This is bizarre. It's like we're in a totally different world."

Pete, who had been rather quiet as they ate, spoke up. "I think it's exactly that, and we must have somehow fallen into another universe. I have read about scientists saying there may be other universes out there. I've never seen any proof, but it seems to be the only explanation that fits the facts. Unless of course, we are all dreaming!"

The boys tried to tell the sisters about their world, but it was all so different, and the girls' language didn't have words for some of the things in the other world, so they soon gave up.

"You don't have cars or trains?" asked Nat.

"I don't understand what you mean," said Brecky.

"Cars are machines with wheels and engines that people ride in to get from one place to another. Trains are another kind of machine that runs on metal rails."

Brecky laughed. "How strange! We have horses and carts or wagons if we want to go far, but we mostly walk. And what do you mean by engines?"

"Engines are things we build to make our stuff work." Seeing Brecky's puzzled expression, Nat shrugged his shoulders. "Never mind. It's too hard to explain."

"Do you live on this beach?" asked Will.

"No, our farm is up there." Lanya pointed to the cliff, then to the left. "Not too far away is our closest town Estaria on the river Staria."

She pointed the other way, "That way is the small seaport of Altara. Ships bring trade goods from farther south, like woven fabrics, iron, and tools, but we've never been there."

"I did my first mind meld with a southern trader. My mother showed me how," Brecky said.

"One of the sailors said they don't go north because the sea is dangerous with nasty monsters." Izzy shivered. "If he was telling the truth, many sailors have never come back from sailing there."

"Some who managed the journey came back with stories of ruins and relics of old cities."

Brecky replied, "We have a few tales about the old days.

Now I think about it, they may have been something like you say your world is now. People say horrible wars and many disasters made a lot of land disappear into the ground in massive earthquakes, and great big waves caused floods which covered all the low land. So many people died that hardly anything remained of their time. At least that's what the old tales say. Nobody knows much about their history, although parts of a few buildings have survived on the higher mountain slopes. But it was supposed to be thousands and even millions of years ago."

Izzy said, "We get some of the metals we use in our farming when landslides uncover buried items."

Lanya jumped into the conversation. "Our father found strange writing on skins after a landslide near our farm revealed holes in the rock. He was convinced they were clues to the old days and was fascinated by the sailors' tales. He set off with a friend over a year ago to look.

"Our dad travels a lot too," said Will.

"Where is your father now?" asked Pete.

"We don't know. He disappeared one day. Our mother was able to keep in touch with him for a long time by scrying." Brecky looked off into the distance.

"What's scrying?" interrupted Nat.

"Our mother, like many others, can see someone far away. She gets a mirror or a bowl of water and when she thinks very hard about someone, she can see them in the water or mirror. She can see part of where they are but can't speak to them," Lanya replied.

Nat had a knowing look. "You must be right, Pete. We *are* in an alternate universe. Nothing else can explain all this." He gestured around him.

"But how did we all get here and why?" asked Will.

"I had those strange feelings even before we got to the cottage. It's like I was being called to that cave. And Becky was too," said Pete.

Simple, Peter. It was time for me to hatch, and I needed you from your world, so I called you here together with Brecchettya.

"Why and for what?" he asked.

It is a long story, and I am feeling very tired. I will go back into the cave to rest.

"But—" cried Pete to her back.

She ignored him as she went to the cave.

"It's no use trying to get anything out of her now, but there's obviously a lot more to this mystery, and we won't solve it without her." Brecky shook her head.

"I wonder what time it is." Nat looked at his phone. "Strange, that can't be right. We've been here much longer than that. Weird! And I forgot to call Mum. She'll be worrying."

"What is that funny thing?" Brecky pointed to his phone.

"It's the way we talk to each other across long distances."

"Like a scry?" Lanya asked.

"Sort of, but we can actually talk to the person," Nat explained.

"I wonder if we'll be able to return tomorrow." Pete looked sadly at the lapping waves.

"Always supposing we can get back home," Will said gloomily.

You will.

It was going to take Pete a while to get used to the dragon speaking in his head. He glanced at the others, but no one else seemed to have heard her.

I can choose to speak privately to anyone I want to. I have a group voice and a private voice.

"Jessynta seems to think we will," Pete told the others. "So let's meet here tomorrow."

"If we can—and that is a big *if*," said Nat.

"Don't be such a plonker. Have faith. I have a very strong feeling that we will. We are at the beginning of a really fantastic adventure." He turned to the girls. "Maybe tomorrow we can talk more about Avalanya, and we'll try to explain a bit more about our world."

The three boys said goodbye to their new friends and went into the cave. Jessynta's glowing scales faintly lit her surroundings as she curled up in a corner.

As the best climber, Nat went up first, followed very closely by Will who wasn't going to be left behind. Pete was dragging his heels. He really didn't want to leave and took a longing look down at the sleeping dragon. Pushing the fronds at the entrance away, he climbed out slowly.

"What a day!" said Nat happily. "I'm quite relieved we got out of the cave safely."

"It was amazing, fun, and scary at the same time," said Will. "I thought we'd had it once or twice, especially when Jessynta hatched. But I agree, she turned out to be really sweet." He smiled broadly as he thought back to their meeting.

"Look!" Pete pointed back to where they had just been. "The rock turned solid!"

"Knew it," said Nat with a look of disgust and a bit of dismay. "Tomorrow it will all be a memory, and we won't ever get back."

"No," said Pete. "I trust Jessynta, and I believe tomorrow when we come back, it will be open again. Besides, I still feel a slight buzzing in my head like something is in there. I think she's still in contact with me somehow. Before we go, we had better put some twigs and leaves on top of the rope and undo it from the tree. Someone might find it or trip." They covered the rope. "There you are. That shows that we shall be able to go down again."

"Humpf," grunted Nat.

They raced each other back to the cottage. "Hi, Mum!" said Will. "Sorry we've been away so long. What's for tea? We're starving."

"You can't be. Surely you've only just eaten your snacks.

What have you been up to in so short a time that made you so hungry? You look a little tired."

They gazed at each other and then at the time. Sure enough, less than an hour had passed since they had left that morning. Pete thought quickly and whispered to Will. "I think I know, but I'll explain later." To his mother he said. "Well, we do get very hungry. It must be the sea air."

"Must be. Help yourselves to food. I thought we could go down to the beach if you feel like it. You can tell me what you did this morning, and we can visit the center that explains about this area and why it's called the Jurassic Coast."

The boys looked slyly at each other, then Pete said, "That's a good idea. We'll go and get ready." He raced upstairs, followed by the others.

In his room, Pete quickly had a word with the other two. "We will have to be careful what we say as we obviously can't tell her exactly what we've been doing. She'd think we were crazy."

After a quick lunch, they walked past shops and a massive car park to the center, which was housed in a large building between the car park and the entrance to the beach. The boys were fascinated by the pictures and interactive displays showing how the cove had been formed over 10,000 years ago by the power of the sea.

Pete drew Nat aside and whispered in his ear. "Something like that must have happened in Avalanya. It must have taken years and years there too."

Walking on further, a video display outlined millions of years of the Earth's history.

"Just look at the cliffs in those photos. They all have wavy layers in them," said Nat.

"It looks like a giant was playing with Play-Doh and put lots of different layers on top of each other. Then something squished them or ran into them," said Will.

"That's a good description," said their mother. "This whole area was once underwater, and lots of layers of rocks settled on the ocean floor, burying early sea creatures. Land movement molded them, and they shifted up and down with earthquakes. It took millions and millions of years, and when the sea receded, the rocks were left in those shapes. It also buried the early creatures like the dinosaurs. Will, perhaps you could do some research into geology and what causes the earth to move like that."

Will went forward to have a closer look at the pictures. "Hey, Pete, that sounds like what must have happened in Ava— Ouch!" He rubbed his foot where Pete had stomped on it.

"Sorry," said Pete. "I was looking at those pictures of that funny archway called Durdle Door and wasn't looking where I was going. Come and look at them."

He dragged Will away from their mother's earshot. "You nearly said something about where we've been. You must be more careful. You're lucky Mum didn't hear."

"Mum, can we go look for those wavy rocks?" Nat asked.

"We don't have enough time this afternoon, but we can go to the top of the cliff and look from a distance."

Behind the center, they climbed steep, wide steps to be rewarded with a fantastic view from the top. They looked over the cove resembling a horseshoe. The path continued past an open field to a sign for the footpath and an arrow pointing to the right. They followed the path to the edge of a cliff and saw a very steep path leading down to the beach.

"Can we go down there?" asked Will eagerly.

"I just told you, we don't have enough time today, but we can always come back another day if you like."

"Yes, we like exploring, don't we?" Will looked at the others with a smirk.

Back in their cottage, Pete said, "That was really interesting, Mum. Thanks a lot. I don't think we'll have any trouble enjoying ourselves in this place, what with everything we've done so far." The boys grinned broadly behind their mother's back.

"I'm pleased you're excited about it here. You may also be pleased that your father might be here later tonight after all, and we have a surprise planned for the day after next, so you better get more exploring done tomorrow as we shall be out most of the next day."

As they went off to bed, Pete said, "I wonder what their surprise is. It couldn't possibly as exciting as what we're going to do tomorrow."

"If we can get to Avalanya again," said Nat.

"You're a proper spoilsport. I told you not to worry. I can still feel Jessynta in my mind."

CHAPTER FOUR

"GOOD MORNING, BOYS," SAID their father when they rushed into the kitchen. "Unusual for all three of you to be up so early. You must have planned an exciting day, and I suppose you'll be too busy to chill out with your father."

"Morning! I didn't hear you come in," said Pete.

Nat said, "Mum told us you have arranged something for us to do together tomorrow, so we thought we'd explore around here today. You don't mind, do you?"

"No, not at all. I've been so busy at work, I'll be glad for a day of leisure."

The boys gobbled down a substantial breakfast, said goodbye, and left.

Finding the rope where they had hidden it, they tied it to the tree again. Nat went to the rock and parted the concealing fronds.

"Knew it!" he exclaimed in disgust. "Solid rock."

"Let me see," said Pete. As he spoke and touched the rock, it shimmered and dissolved. Startled, he stumbled backward as he was hit by an almost overwhelming wave of excitement.

I was worried about you. I felt you somewhere far away. I have come to this end of the tunnel every day and called for you!

Pete climbed down carefully, closely followed by his brothers.

Two large, clawed forepaws encircled him.

"Hi, Jessynta. It's good to see you too, but we've only been gone one night. My goodness, you 've grown an awful lot. You're more the size of a small pony now! How could that have happened?"

One night? But it has been at least fourteen sleeps! And we grow during the night. She hung her head sadly. *Oh, I forgot time works differently in your universe. Silly me, I should have remembered, but it has been so many thousands of years since my mother laid my egg and told me about it.*

"Stop right there," cried Pete. "Let's get into daylight and talk about this new stuff."

When they exited the cave, they were almost immediately joined by the three girls.

"Are you happy now, Jessynta?" Brecky asked. To the boys, she added, "We're glad to see you too. She has been doing nothing but eating and growing. It did get easier these last few days when she got big enough to fish for herself."

Well, that is why having two bond mates is better to look after my needs. Having Izchettya and Guillanya helped a great deal.

"She is using their formal Avalanyan names," explained Brecky before they could ask.

"Tell us what you meant by saying you should have remembered?" asked Nat. "You only just got out of the shell, so you couldn't possibly have anything to remember."

Do you not have genetic memory?

With a puzzled expression, Pete said, "I know what genetics are: characteristics inherited from our parents. But genetic memory? We all start as tiny babies and learn everything from scratch. We can't talk and don't even know our own names. Our mothers choose a name for us, and we gradually learn it as we begin to talk."

Not too convenient. Dragons have our mother's memories

from when we first started in the egg, and our mother gives us our name before we hatch.

"You said time was different in our universe. How can we calculate how much time has passed in the different places?"

That is a bit tricky, as it is not always the same and it varies. It can be as much as one month of ours to only a few days of yours. However, I am not very sure about that or how to work it out.

"I suppose we just have to guess. In any case, we wouldn't be able to stay here longer than one of our days, or our parents will really get worried. We'll have to be careful," said Nat.

Jessynta was silent for a few minutes.

I might be able to adjust things as I recall more of my genetic memories, so you can stay longer without too much time going past in your world. It would only involve a bit of magic. Anything is possible if you try hard enough. I think it has something to do with my eggshell pieces.

Will sighed, holding both hands to his face. "After the scrying thing Brecky says her mother does, and the whole mind-melding thing, it shouldn't be surprising to hear you can manipulate time too."

"Why did you pick a bond mate from our universe?" Pete asked the dragon.

My ancestors knew of your world from its early years and watched over its development. It is unique among worlds, Jessynta explained.

Pete's mouth dropped open. "Why?"

Because it has so much variety and many different species of animals and plant life. More than anywhere else.

Brecky frowned. "We have horses, dogs, birds, and wild animals too."

Yes, and in the old days, there many more, although not as diverse as Pete's world. Where we are now was once part of a huge continent with high mountain ranges. Those islands in the south are merely the tops of some of them. The rest are under the sea.

Izzy grabbed Brecky's arm. "We've heard tales that there were once big cities with tall buildings."

Girls, it might surprise you to know that the tales you have heard are not far from the truth.

Brecky gasped in surprise. "You mean those tales we've heard are for real?"

"Did they have big machines which could fly?" said Izzy.

Yes, this island was once part of a huge continent with high mountain ranges, and those islands out there in the ocean are really just the tops of them. The rest are under the sea.

"And they lived in big cities with really tall buildings?" asked Lanya.

According to my mother's memories, the people made the air bad everywhere and cut down large areas of forest and jungle causing hundreds of animals to become extinct from a lack of food. They used up their resources, so they were unable to replace their machinery when it wore out. Devastating wars were fought over what was left and much more was destroyed. More trees were cut down, causing famine and erosion. They continued building bigger and bigger cities causing the air to become so polluted that people became ill. The world gradually got hotter and hotter.

Pete's mouth fell open, and his eyes opened wide as he turned to his brothers. "That's way too much like what's happening in our world right now."

Enormous storms and the seas flooded almost every bit of low-lying land. Some countries had no rain at all, and nothing could grow. Many animals could not survive, and thousands of people died as a result.

Dragons also suffered from a lack of food. Violent earthquakes forced us to leave our lands. Few people survived, and their civilization practically died out. Humans blamed us for some of it, but my mother's memories are sparse about that part.

"That sounds scary. Our scientists say our world is getting warmer too," said Nat.

Pete stared out over the water. "Those problems are often in the news in our world, and scientists are always talking about global warming, but some people don't agree with them or about the solution. Many grown-ups, including our parents, are worried that something might happen in the future to us like what seems to have happened to you here."

I believe that is one of the reasons you have been brought here. I hope you will be able to help our world recover and to stop it from happening in your world. You need to tell everyone there about how our world lost everything. The last remaining dragons, including my mother, laid eggs to wait for the future when maybe something could be done.

"Is that why we don't have any records of the past?" asked Brecky. "I suppose they got destroyed."

"In any case," put in Lanya, "even if there were records, we're too busy working on the farms to study old text. Not much of the old language is written down, and only the cleverest among us are able to translate what we have, so nobody is really sure if any of it is true."

Nat frowned. "Jessynta, where are the other dragon eggs?"

They could be anywhere. I believe I am sensing one getting ready to hatch. Your first task will be to locate and awaken the other dragons. I am not absolutely certain where or what species they are.

"It really is true about the history of our world then," said Brecky. "It isn't a myth."

Of course. After all, we are real.

Suddenly, Pete and Brecky clutched their stomachs. Pete exclaimed, "I'm absolutely starving. We rushed out in such a hurry, we completely forgot to bring any food with us."

Brecky moaned. "I'm starved too."

Oh, I am sorry. You are bonded to me, and I am really hungry.

Izzy said, "No worries. We live close. Lanya and I can easily run home for food. Jessynta, are you able to get a few fish for us?"

Of course.

Pete, Will, and Nat gathered driftwood to make a fire. They were looking for flint stones to spark a fire when Jessynta returned with a load of fish in a net borrowed from the girls.

You do not have to light a fire in that primitive way. I can light a fire.

"Then do it or we'll be eating that fish raw," Pete said. "Oh thank goodness. Here they come."

In a few minutes, Jessynta had lit the fire, the fish was cooking, and the meal was spread out on the beach.

The food was delicious. There was the same fresh-baked bread, butter, and cheese as before, as well as a few different dishes.

"This orange spread tastes a bit like our hummus, doesn't it?" said Pete.

"Sure does." Nat dipped his bread into the paste and took a large bite.

Jessynta bit into the prepared fish. *It is edible, but I like it better raw.*

"Will you tell us more about genetic memory, Jessynta?" asked Pete.

Our mothers talk to us as the egg grows inside her and even more after the egg is laid. She told me everything she could remember about the world as she knew it and even passed on her mother's knowledge. Mind you, even though it is all in my mind, I have to search around for much of it. It will take time for me to get it all straight.

"Stunning. I would never have imagined that could happen. That does sound useful, but we don't have anything like that." Pete looked at his brothers.

They shook their heads.

"What about dragons? We have loads of myths too. Do you know if they ever existed in our world?" asked Will eagerly.

No, they did not, , but it is another long story, so you will have to contain your curiosity a bit longer.

Jessynta lifted her snout toward the distant island.

I can sense an egg not too far from here. It seems to be on that island which used to be part of a mountain range. It should be ready to hatch quite soon. I will rely on you to locate its exact position when we get closer. I have told it we will be coming. It is up to them to choose which of you they want, just like I chose Peter and Brechettya.

"Do dragons choose us then and not the other way around?" asked Will.

Yes, that is correct. Each of the dragons will be bonded to an Earthling and an Avalanyan.

"If we're going to the island, we'll need a small boat," Brecky said.

"Let's get ours. It's in the cove just around the headland," Izzy pointed to the edge of the bay. "There's a narrow footpath we have to climb. At the top, the path divides. One way leads back to our village, and the other leads down to a rocky ledge where we keep our boat."

I am a water dragon, and although I can climb a little, it is much easier for me to swim around the headland and meet you on the other side. I have yet to develop enough magical skills to move with ease on land or even in the air.

Jessynta waddled out to the sea and disappeared into the waves.

"What do you suppose she meant by developing magical skills?" asked Pete.

Lanya replied, "Many of our people know a little magic."

"Now why doesn't that surprise me?" Nat smirked.

"We are familiar with minor magic, and a few can use it to

help with their healing remedies. My mother and Aunt Suki use herbs for healing."

"Nobody can perform magic of any kind where we come from, although there are some magicians who pretend they can," said Pete.

Following the girls, the boys climbed the narrow footpath. At the top, Lanya stopped, sweeping her arm to take in the valley below. "Those wheat fields are ours, and there are our fruit trees. If you look hard into the distance, you'll see our farmhouse."

The footpath forked with one way leading to a small group of houses on the banks of an estuary.

"That is Estaria, our village. We'll go down there another day. Our boat is this way, moored to a stone jetty." Brecky led the way.

"Is that Jessynta swimming toward it?" asked Will.

"Unless you know another water dragon, that's a good guess," Izzy laughed.

Jessynta broke the surface as the children reached the jetty.

"Hi, Jessynta," called Brecky. "Can you hold it steady for us to climb in?"

Will looked at the rocking boat skeptically. "I can swim but make sure you hold it tight for me, Jessynta."

Do not worry, Will. If you should fall in, I can easily rescue you.

When Will didn't seem reassured, Pete and Nat held out their hands to steady him. They all climbed in and settled in their seats.

Hold tight. I am going to push you.

Will closed his eyes and held onto his brothers. Nat said, "It's great not to have to row."

You need to save your energy for the next part of the journey as it might be hard going.

"Look, Will! You can see the rooftops of Estaria on either side of the estuary," said Lanya.

Will slowly opened his eyes to look around. Relaxing, he let go of his brothers.

"We must be nearly there," said Brecky. "There are a lot of little islands, so let's start searching for somewhere to land. Where do you think the egg might be, Jessynta? And where can we moor our boat? It looks quite deep and rocky."

I will swim ahead and look more closely.

Suddenly, Nat grabbed his head. "I hear something; it's a voice calling me, and it's very anxious. Something is up there, and it says to get a move on."

Jessynta swam back to them.

I see a possible landing spot, but it might be difficult to get there, as lots of rocks are just under the surface. You will have to be very careful. Sit still and I will nudge you in. It is shallow enough here that I can touch the bottom, so I will hold the boat as you climb out onto that rock.

She gently pushed them close to the flat rock, then held the boat steady. Brecky and Pete tied the boat to a half-submerged tree stump.

"Look, Nat," said Will, happy to be on land again. "Wavy rocks just like those we saw yesterday."

But Nat was pacing the area in agitation. "Don't distract me with wavy rocks. He's been expecting us, but he says to hurry. He's so very loud."

"I can hear him too. He's calling from over there." Izzy pointed to the rocks Will was inspecting.

This area was once an extremely high mountain. The sea flooded most of it. You should be able to climb to the top, and that is where he will be, as he is an air dragon, not a water dragon like me. Air dragons lay their eggs on the top of a sheer cliff to keep them safe.

"The rocks are almost like shallow steps so that should help. Here's your chance to climb, Nat. It's a good thing our mother isn't here." Pete laughed.

"Izzy likes climbing, too." Brecky held up a bundle. "Let's take this rope from the boat, just in case."

Good thinking, young Brecchettya. Nathaniel and Izchettya should lead, and the rest of us will follow. Perhaps two of you can help me, as I am not as good at climbing as I am at swimming.

The children roped themselves together. Luckily, it wasn't too steep, and landslides had formed slopes. Moving carefully, they didn't slip much, but their progress was slow.

"The dragon is very excited," said Nat.

"It's hard to concentrate with him chirping at us constantly," said Izzy.

"Jessynta, I thought you said the air dragons laid their eggs on a sheer cliff so nobody could disturb them; this seems more like a slope," Pete said.

There have been many storms and landslides over the centuries, so in this case, they have helped us.

They reached a flat shelf jutting out from the edge. After a bit of a scramble, they climbed onto it. A cave sat toward the back of the shelf against the mountainside.

I'll stay outside and under the shelf as it is a little narrow for me, but remember, Nathaniel and Izchettya must touch the egg first in order to complete the bond.

Inside, a large oval object glowed a luminous mottled green. It was almost twice the size Jessynta's egg had been, and a tiny, jagged hole pierced the top.

Izzy and Nat moved closer to the egg and carefully laid their hands on it. They experienced a blinding flash of light and tingling, much like Pete and Brecky had described.

Oh, at last you are here! I have been waiting for this day for so long. I thought it would never come. I am Edwith, and I am so happy to feel you near me at last.

"Nice to meet you, Edwith," Izzy said politely.

"Me too. What do you need us to do?" asked Nat.

I can tell there are more of you, and everyone can help me get out of this egg. I seem to have been in it for such a long time. This shell is extra tough, and I am really cramped.

"Can you help us?" Izzy asked the others.

They all pulled and pulled and pulled but nothing happened.

What are you doing? Why can you not pull my shell open? I will push with my paws to see if I can help from inside.

Two small cracks opened on either side, and two rather wet front claws pushed out, followed by a head through the top. Suddenly two more holes appeared on the sides near the bottom and out came hind feet. The dragon attempted to stand which caused him to overbalance.

He bounced around like a ball with legs, trying to break out of the shell. The children burst into laughter. The dragon joined in the laughter and played to their delighted amusement, bouncing around the smooth rock edge.

Gather the egg shards, children, Jessynta said.

The end of a spiked tail burst through the bottom, and Edwith came to a stop, rocking slightly. As he tried to balance on the end of his tail, he twisted unexpectedly to the left and pivoted on his tail spike. Before anyone could stop him, he spun around like a top.

He shrieked with surprise and then delight. *I say! This is great fun. Yippee! Yippee!*

"Did you hear that? He sounds like quite a clown," said Will.

The others nodded, laughing.

Yes, you can hear him because you touched him when you helped him open the shell.

There was no stopping him, as round and round he spun, faster and faster. They laughed loudly at his antics.

For goodness sake, stop laughing at him, children! You will only make him worse, Jessynta shouted.

At that moment, Edwith completely overbalanced and tumbled over the edge of the shelf.

EDWITH

CHAPTER FIVE

HORROR-STRUCK, NAT CLAMBERED DOWN off the shelf, closely followed by Izzy who was white as a sheet. They caught sight of the dragon tumbling ungainly head over paws, over tail, over wings, in a complete tangle, as he rolled and skidded down the sloping side of the mountain. He finally came to a stop upside down amongst chunks of debris and shell at the bottom.

Nat and Izzy almost fell themselves, scrambling down to get to him. As they got closer, they heard the strangest sounds coming from him.

"Oh no, he must be hurt. What's the matter?" Nat rushed to soothe him.

The sounds grew even louder with gasps.

"I don't think he's hurt. He's laughing!" said Izzy as the sounds got clearer.

There is nothing wrong with him at all. The cheeky creature is having fun, said Jessynta.

The other four children came down slowly, gathering eggshells as they went, helping Jessynta and arriving to Edwith's howls of laughter.

Edwith picked himself up and, shaking the rest of the shell fragments off his body, looked himself over. *I am not hurt. I have a very thick skin, but I do feel a little shaky. No harm done, and I did get out of my shell, did I not?*

"Thank goodness for that," said Nat.

"I really ought to get mad at you for frightening the life out of me," said Izzy.

In addition to the fact that you scared the humans, that was a shameful display of bad behavior from a dragon, said Jessynta.

So sorry, ma'am. A lop-sided grin spread over Edwith's jaws, and he lowered his head.

Now that they were all relieved and settled, they had a good look at him.

"You really are very handsome with all the colors of the rainbow on your hide, and you're already almost as large as Jessynta. In fact, you're almost the size of a small pony. I hope we'll be able to fit you in our boat," said Izzy.

He preened himself in delight, shaking the long green tendrils around his face and raising a green crest on his head. His horns were long and green as well. His back had a spine of spikes, and his large, multi-colored, scaly wings folded tightly to his sides. As they watched in fascination, he opened his wings to an extremely large span with more luminous scales.

His tail was spiked at the end, and his body very muscular, though his coloring was difficult to determine. The overall look was one of pale green that almost matched the sky above them, but the scales were shot through with the colors of the rainbow. As he twisted and stretched in delight at his new freedom, he was constantly changing color.

Welcome, young Edwith. Now that you have calmed down a little, try to stay that way so we can all get down to the shore without further mishaps. I mean that, Edwith! Then we will see what can be done about feeding you. Children, bring the shards of the shell.

As they collected the shells, Edwith greeted them again, insisting on hugging each one, nearly knocking Nat and Izzy over, and then they made their way to the waiting boat.

This place is such fun! I can slide. He promptly tried to skate on the rubble, managing to slip several times as he clowned around.

Edwith, please behave. I know you are excited, but we have a long way to go, and the longer you mess about, the longer it will be before we can give you some food.

That sobered him up at once, and he waited while Jessynta swam out to get fish.

"It's going to be a little tricky finding enough food to satisfy a creature that big," said Nat.

I suppose you will not be very keen on fish. Jessynta presented Edwith with a wriggling pile. *But these should fill you until we can get back to the mainland and locate something more to your liking.*

He snorted. *You are right there. But it is kind of you, and I do not mind a little bit of fish. It is good for my brain. And of course, I am going to be very clever.*

Now then, young Edwith, not so much of the boasting. You have a lot to learn.

Oh, I know that, but I learn very quickly. You will see. Edwith promptly wolfed down the fish and released a humongous burp. *Excuse me, but I was absolutely starving!*

Well now. The boat is going to be a bit crowded, so I have an idea. Peter and Brechettya can ride on my back, and then there will be room enough for Edwith, unless he wants to swim.

I am not going to get in the water.

It turned out to be very hard to get the large, ungainly dragon into the boat. In his eagerness, he nearly upended it several times. Luckily Jessynta was able to keep it fairly steady. At last they settled down with Edwith in the bottom of the boat sitting between Izzy, Nat, Lanya, and Will, leaving Pete and Brecky on the rock to wait for Jessynta.

After Jessynta had guided the boat out into the open water away from the rocks and ordered Edwith sternly to sit still, she returned to get Pete and Brecky. They climbed on her back—

no mean feat as her scales were quite slippery—but they held the frill around her neck.

Hold on tight.

They set off with Jessynta pushing the boat, and all was calm for a time.

Edwith said, *I think I am going to throw up.*

As he struggled to get to the side of the boat, it started to tip. Hastily, while Nat and Izzy grabbed him, Will and Lanya scrambled to the other side of the boat to balance it.

"Edwith, stop that or you'll tip the boat over!" shouted Nat.

Behave yourself, Edwith. Control yourself at once. You must remember your responsibilities as a dragon. You have humans in the boat with you, and I will not have you overturning it. They could drown!

He calmed down after those stern words from Jessynta. Even so, the trip back was a little hair-raising as Edwith, after he had recovered from his initial sickness, got so excited, he nearly overturned the boat again.

I just told you, Edwith, you must stop this behavior at once or I will throw you overboard.

Sorry. I really cannot help being excited. You do not know how long I spent cooped up in that horrid shell.

I, too, spent a long time in my shell, and you will just have to be patient. We are trying to help you, so sit still and be quiet! The calmer you are, the sooner we will get there.

After a little more grumbling about why he found it hard to contain himself, he settled down, and soon they were in reach of where they usually moored the boat. A strange boy waved to them from the landing spot.

"That looks like our cousin Ven. He lives in the village near the beach," exclaimed Brecky.

They landed the boat and greeted Ven, who was absolutely struck dumb when he saw the two dragons with them.

"Hallo, Ven. Meet our new friends," said Brecky.

Ven rubbed his eyes in amazement. "Where did you find those creatures? I thought dragons were a myth."

Brecky said, "That's what we thought. It's quite a long story. We helped them hatch."

Ven continued to stare in awe.

"We also want you to meet Pete, Nat, and Will. They're strangers from another world," Brecky said with a mischievous grin on her face.

Ven roared with laughter.

"Don't do that. It's true. We had to do a mind meld with them, but at least now we can understand each other."

"Oh, Mother has done that before for strangers passing through. They had fair hair like that boy, but not long enough to pull back." Ven gestured at the brothers.

Izzy looked around. "How did you get here? It's quite a walk from where you live."

"I borrowed a pony from Father. It's up there in the field. As it's such a nice day, I had thought we might go for a ride, but I guess with all this excitement, we won't be able to."

I will leave you to talk to this boy then, and I will swim back to the cove and meet you there.

Hey, what about me? asked Edwith.

You have a choice. You can either swim with me or climb the path with everyone else.

What? Me swim? Not on your life. What do you think I am, a fish? I suppose I will have to climb, but I may need help.

"We'll help you," Izzy said.

Ven looked puzzled. "Who are you talking to?"

"Jessynta, the blue dragon, says she's going to swim around to our cove on the other side of the headland," said Izzy.

"But Edwith doesn't like the water and won't swim," added Nat.

"I didn't hear anything." Ven looked back and forth between the dragons.

"Sorry, Ven. We'll try to tell you at least some of the story while we help Edwith up the cliff path."

Please let us get going. I am bored with all this chit chat, said Edwith.

As they all helped Edwith, they explained as much as they could to Ven.

"So you actually hear the dragons in your mind? Why can't I?" asked Ven.

"We can try to sort that with Jessynta when she joins us. You have to touch them both, I think," said Brecky.

"That sounds scary."

"No, not at all. We'll show you. Isn't that your pony in the field?"

Ven's pony waited in the field, munching at the high grass. At their approach, it took one look at the dragon and ran away.

Ven ran after it, calling for it to come back.

What a pity. He looked so good to eat.

"No, no! Edwith, this is a tame animal, and you can't eat the tame ones. They're like friends to us. Besides, he belongs to Ven here," said Nat.

Oh dear, what am I going to eat then? This is all going to be more complicated than I imagined. Edwith hung his head.

Izzy said, "Don't worry, you won't have to starve. There are animals you can eat. We'll show you them later But now we have to go down the other side to the beach."

He brightened up considerably, soon returning to his clownish self as they urged him on.

Ven gave up on the pony and rejoined the group.

It was a lot easier getting Edwith down to the beach on the other side of the hill, as he simply sat down and slid, rolling over and over, again making them laugh.

When he reached the bottom, he stood and shook the dust off his hide. *I do not know that I am so keen on being out of my shell now with all this work. Where is this food you talked about?*

Jessynta came up from the sea to greet them with very large fish for Edwith who gulped them down whole, burping loudly.

"This seems to be giving everyone a lot of amusement but you still haven't said how you can get me to hear the dragons." Ven poked Brecky in the ribs.

"Ouch! Don't do that. I'll ask Jessynta."

Ven stood very still, staring hard at Jessynta and Edwith

Tell him to come close to me and put his hands on my muzzle, and I will speak to him. She lowered her head close to Ven.

Ven looked a little scared but did as Brecky told him.

Hallo, Zarven. Pleased to meet you. I am able to speak to anyone, but it seems more polite to wait until they agree through contact.

"I really can hear her! You weren't kidding me. But why Zarven? All my friends call me Ven."

Names are very special to dragons. We almost never shorten them. Come here, Edwith, and introduce yourself to Zarven.

Edwith excitedly charged up to Ven so fast, he tripped over his feet, knocking Ven down and accidentally making the contact. Ven screamed.

I am sorry. Are you all right? I am so clumsy. He hung his head.

Ven looked as though he didn't know whether to laugh or cry. "I'm fine. You scared me is all, but I can hear you now. It's quite amazing."

Everyone began talking at once.

Edwith interrupted them. *I am sure you are all having fun, but I am still really hungry. That fish was not quite enough for me, although I do thank you, Jessynta, for your kindness. I am not quite strong enough yet to go hunting for myself.*

"My goodness, so you must be, a huge creature like you, but what are we going to give you to eat?" said Nat.

"I think we'll have to get our bows and arrows and shoot some game. There should be wild deer in that forest over there." Izzy pointed into the trees.

The boys were open-mouthed.

Nat said, "We couldn't do that. I don't think I'd feel very comfortable killing a creature."

"How do you eat where you come from then?" asked Izzy. "We learn to shoot from a very young age, otherwise we'd starve."

"We're mostly vegetarian in our family, so we don't eat meat at all, but we do eat eggs, cheese, and other kinds of food we can make or buy in the supermarkets, and lots and lots of fruit, nuts, and veggies," said Pete. "Although a lot of people do eat meat, they usually buy it ready to cook."

"It sounds as though you live a very different life from ours. Is a supermarket like our weekly markets in the square?" asked Brecky.

This is still not getting me any closer to food, said Edwith.

I should have warned you that humans love to talk. They would talk nonstop if they could, said Jessynta.

The children laughed at Jessynta's words.

"Why don't Brecky and I find food for Edwith?" said Lanya.

By the time the girls returned carrying a large deer between them, Ven was sitting quietly, thinking about all he had heard and seen. He stared at the two dragons.

"It may be time for us to return to our world. I have no idea how much time has passed there, but it does seem that we've been here longer this time, what with the boat trip and all." Pete stood and brushed the sand from his trousers. "Mum has something special planned for us tomorrow, so we'll be making an early start."

"Oh no," said Nat. "I'd forgotten all about that. We can come here before we go, can't we?"

"I don't think there will be enough time. They want to start off early." Pete looked downcast. "We'll have to wait until we get home from the trip."

Nat's face fell. "But that could be very late; we don't know where they're taking us."

Oh dear, moaned Edwith, looking up in the middle of tearing lumps off the deer. *I only just met you, and now you are talking about going away again. Where are you going?*

"We aren't from here. The girls will explain once we're gone." Nat stroked Edwith's snout.

Jessynta had been rather quiet for a while, but now she spoke up. *Avalanyan bond mates can help us during your necessary absences. I think there may be a solution to make our separation times shorter. Edwith, search your memories. I just know those shell pieces are important somehow.*

Their mothers used to hold on to pieces of dragonet shells to keep an eye on them when they went off to play, said Edwith excitedly.

Peter and Nathaniel, take pieces of the shells back to your world. Perhaps the shell will act as a conduit back to here and give us the ability to hold a short conversation, said Jessynta.

"How will it work?" asked Pete.

Hold a small piece in your hand and concentrate on us. But you will have to use them sparingly as each piece may only be used once. I think, unless I am mistaken, that using the shell pieces might alter the time, keeping us more in sync. Do not get too excited, as it may not work with you in a different world. I will search my memories for a different method of communication, but for now, use the shells.

"I completely agree. We need time to get to know each other, but I suppose I have to agree with Pete," said Nat sadly.

Pete put eggshell pieces in his pocket. "We'll try the shells to see what happens."

"If they work," Nat whispered to Will.

I do not like this arrangement at all.

"Nor do I, but Izzy will be here to help you," said Nat.

"We'll be sure to feed him lots and lots of good meat, so he'll soon be very strong," said Izzy.

Okay! Food sounds good. Edwith jumped in excitement,

losing his balance and ending upside down. *It is time for a nap.*

"We're going to find you a nice cave after the boys have gone," Izzy said.

"Pete, are you sure we need to go right now? I really want to stay a bit longer and help Edwith find a nice place to sleep."

"I'm afraid time's up."

Nat said, "We can't have been here that long."

You should listen to your brother. My inner sense tells me he is right. And you are upsetting Edwith! Look at him. Jessynta flung her wing out in the younger dragon's direction.

Nat looked at him and saw that Edwith was indeed hesitating. "Jessynta, even you're taking sides. It's not fair."

"It probably isn't, but this is how it has to work," said Pete.

Jessynta nodded her head.

Reluctantly, Nat gave Edwith a big, tearful hug, said goodbye to Jessynta, the girls, and Ven. He picked up the bag of shells and started off toward the cave.

Will followed at his heels. "Do you think we can talk to any Avalanyan now, like we talked to Ven? Just one mind meld and it works with everyone?"

"That's how I understand it," Pete said.

Before Nat entered the cave, he looked back at Edwith who was turning somersaults for the girls, making them and Ven laugh.

Reassured, Nat followed his brothers. Pete climbed up first, and much to everybody's relief, the rock opened up, and outside everything looked unaltered. After they had climbed out, the cave's entrance silently closed. Looking back, they saw no trace of it. They once again covered the rope with leaves and twigs and started down the hillside.

When they reached the house, their mother waited at the door looking a little anxious.

"I wondered where you were. I went into the woods at the back to see if I could see you. I thought we could all go for a picnic on the beach this afternoon. What on earth have you been doing up there that's so interesting?"

"Er, well, you know, just rambling around and exploring footpaths," said Pete. "But going to the beach with you sounds fun. Maybe we could have a swim."

After grabbing a snack, the boys went upstairs to find their swimsuits.

"I say, Nat, we really have to tell Mum soon, as she may start to get suspicious. I don't like telling stories to her. It's dishonest, and I feel bad about it."

"She'll never believe us. I almost don't believe it myself." Looking at this phone, Nat said, "That's strange. Last time I looked at my phone, it had a different time."

"I wonder if it's something to do with Avalanya and the time there. And, of course, they don't have any satellites. We'd better leave them to charge. We won't need them anyway; we'll be with Mum and Dad."

CHAPTER SIX

THE BOYS PUT THEIR swimsuits on and grabbed towels.

"Why don't I take a few shell pieces with us in case we get a chance to be alone?" Pete put a few in his backpack and raced the other two down the stairs.

Will noticed their parents were not dressed for a swim. "Aren't you swimming?"

"No, it's not for me. The sea's a bit too cold. I'll just watch you and relax on the beach with Mum," said their father.

The boys splashed around until Will began to shiver. He headed for the beach. "I'm a little cold. Let's play ball now."

The other two readily agreed. After playing ball to warm up, they sat in the sun, away from their parents.

Nat stared into the distance. "I'm finding it so hard to stop thinking about Edwith. I want to try out those shells. I'm dying to see if we can actually talk to the dragons."

"I'm curious myself, but we have to stay longer, or our parents will wonder why we aren't as enthusiastic about being here as we should be," said Pete.

They kicked a ball around a bit more and watched their mum setting out the picnic food. They eagerly went over to help her.

They were busy eating when, through a mouthful of bread and cheese, Will said, "These sandwiches are great. Have you ever tried to bake your own bread, Mum?"

Pete glared at Will, worried he would mention the fresh baked bread they had eaten in Avalanya. "Can I have a drink please, Mum? I'm thirsty."

She opened the picnic basket and gave them each a can.

The rest of the afternoon went by slowly for the boys, especially Nat.

"You're unusually quiet today. What did you do earlier this morning that tired you out so much?" asked their mother.

"We did a lot of running around in the woods," said Will.

"Remember, we're going on a trip tomorrow, so you had better rest up for the remainder of the day."

Will's face brightened. "Let's go spend some of our allowance in those shops."

"I don't feel like trailing around after you three looking at toys or whatever," said their father.

Will gave a sly grin. "Do you mind if we go on our own then? We won't be long."

"Okay, but don't spend too much money on junk food. Off you go, and we'll clear up and meet you at the cottage." Mum shooed them away.

The brothers quickly set off before their parents could change their minds. With a grin on his face, Will poked Nat. "Now wasn't that clever of me? I knew they wouldn't want to come 'round the shops with us. We can find a spot away from everybody, and try the shells."

"Thanks for that, Will." Nat gave his brother a thumbs up. "I want to find out how Edwith is getting on."

"I'm not sure how to go about this shell thing," said Pete, as soon as they had found a quiet corner well away from anyone. "Do we do it together or one at a time?"

"I vote one at a time," said Nat. "You try first, Pete."

Pete held a piece of shell in his hands and concentrated on Jessynta, but nothing happened.

He experimented, holding it in one hand at a time, then together. Still no luck.

Nat looked disgusted. "Told you so. Knew it wouldn't work."

"Hey, wait up," said Will. "Remember how the girls held their hands to our heads in that mind meld? Why don't you try touching your head with the shell?"

Pete looked doubtful but did as Will suggested. "I'm getting something faint coming through. "No, it's just a buzzing sound. Any more brilliant ideas?"

Will refused to give up. "How about speaking out loud? It might make your thoughts clearer. Like soldiers used to do on those old-fashioned walkie-talkies in the movies?"

"That's stupid." But seeing the look of disappointment on Nat's face, Pete decided to give it a try. He held the shell to his head again. "Pete calling! Come in, Jessynta. Ooh, something's happening. It sounds like e….o…e…i.. e…y…ere, but it's just a jumble of sounds. Now it's coming in clearer. I think it starts with hallo. It does seem to be working. Can you hear me? Are you there? It's definitely Jessynta, but some of the consonants are missing. Try again please, Jessynta."

Hello . . . there . . . Peter. . . This . . . hard— than I thought.

"Jessynta, I'm getting you now. Well done. Keep trying and do it very slowly."

Yes, I have it now. I was thinking too fast. I will slow down. I can hear your words in my head as if you were here. Can you hear me now?

"Loud and clear!"

Will and Nat waited impatiently, listening to the one-sided conversation.

Much has happened since you left, but I will tell you all about it next time we meet. Edwith is jumping up and down and pushing me. He wants to talk to Nat.

"Nat, try holding the shell piece to your head like I did."

However, try as he might, Nat was unable to understand

anything from the jumble of words. "Nothing."

It is probably because Edwith is still very newly hatched and a little excitable. I will see if I can help him with my mind.

The next minute, Edwith was much clearer.

I . . . ow . . . r . . . u? . . . ish you could come back.

"At last! That's better. Think more slowly. Are you being fed?"

. . . es the girls are feeding me lots but need . . . elp. Want to choose a cave. Can you come back now?

"We can't, and remember, we can't come tomorrow either," said Nat. "But Jessynta said using the shells might shorten our time distance."

We are busy sorting out a place for Edwith, but he does not like to sleep alone. We are doing our best to keep him happy. Oh dear. It is hard to hold this conversation. I will need more practice.

"Are you losing contact? How much longer can you hold it? Will is grabbing my arm. He wants to say something."

"Don't let her go yet. I haven't been able to hear anything."

"I'm sorry, Will. I was so excited at the thought of talking with the aid of the shell, I completely forgot to give some to you. Better take one of each."

Will grasped the pieces and held them to his head. "Hi, Jessynta. Can you hear me now?"

Yes, William, you are a bit faint, though it might be because you are not bonded to me like Peter. Edwith is having trouble trying to talk to Nathaniel too. It is good to talk to you all, but I am unable to hold on much longer. . . . I am sure to improve with practice. Go . . . by.

Will was disappointed but, shrugging his shoulders, gave his shells back to Pete. "At least I had a chance to try it out for a second."

Pete said, "I wonder if that took anything off our time. We have to get our times more in sync."

"Good thing we weren't near anyone. People hearing us talk with a shell on our head would think us mad. We need to do this behind our house. When are we going to tell Mum and Dad?" Nat asked.

"It's going to be so hard. We must choose our moment carefully. We'll have to get something to show them somehow, but what? Next time we go to Avalanya, the dragons or the girls might have some ideas." Pete crossed his arms across his chest.

"Do you suppose we could take our parents with us and they could see for themselves?" suggested Will.

"Doubt it," said Nat.

"Our parents will be waiting for us, so we'd better get going. Let's buy candy or something, so they won't be suspicious.Can't wait to see their faces when we do tell about the dragons." Spotting an ice cream van, Pete rushed to buy a cone for each of them.

The brothers were finishing their cones as they walked through the door.

"I'm still hungry," said Nat.

Will licked his cone and nodded his head in agreement.

Mum smiled at them. "It was a good day at the beach. You're quite tanned from the sun, but you do look a little tired from all that swimming and tearing around, boys."

"It's all this fresh air and exercise," Pete said. "What's for dinner?"

"Can we help get food ready?" asked Will.

"It's pasta, and it's all done. Just lay the table, get plates, and help yourselves. Don't forget to wash your hands first."

"Oh yummy! Pasta's my favorite." Will ran off to wash his hands, closely followed by the other two.

While they were eating, their mother said, "I haven't seen you playing games on your box since we got here. It just shows you can manage without electronics. You've been outside so much. What have you found to amuse yourselves?"

Nat glanced at his brothers, giving a little shake of his head in warning. "You know. This and that. There's a lot to explore with the beach and all. Where are we going tomorrow, Dad?"

"You'll see. I think you'll enjoy it. Mum planned it before we came down, and you'll have to get up early. We want to leave around eight. It'll take over an hour to get there depending upon traffic. It's a popular place."

~~~~~

"Pete! Wake up! I need to talk to you urgently." Nat shook his brother's shoulder roughly.

"Whatever is the matter with you? It's only five o'clock in the morning and not even light yet."

"I know, but I had an awful dream about Edwith. He was so upset. He didn't want to be on his own. He didn't like the big caves. He didn't want to sleep with Jessynta either. He wanted Izzy and me to sleep with him."

"Come on! It was only a dream. Stop worrying. It's just your imagination. We can't go there in the middle of the night anyway." He turned his face to the wall.

"But it was so real." Tears welled in Nat's eyes.

"Calm down. Izzy will look after him."

"Suppose for some reason she can't."

"Stop going on about it. Remember Jessynta is there too. She'll sort it."

"Can't we go to see them before we leave with Mum and Dad?"

"No, we can't. We wouldn't have time. I don't know what time we'll get back from our outing, but maybe there'll be time then. Please leave me alone. It's too early and I'm still tired." Ignoring Nat, Pete closed his eyes.

Nat couldn't get back to sleep. As soon as the sky began to lighten, he went to ask Will about his dream.

"You woke me up to tell me that," said Will crossly.
~~~~~

"It's easy for you, Will. Wait until you bond with a dragon and see how you feel."

"Do shut up, Nat. Remember how Edwith likes to clown around? He's most likely leading them all in a merry dance!"

Reluctantly, Nat agreed but still looked unhappy.

When the sun broke the horizon, the boys dressed and trooped downstairs to greet their parents who were already up making breakfast.

"Glad you're up early," said their father. "Why the long face, Nat?"

"A bit tired. Didn't sleep too well."

"Well, I hope you're rested enough for an adventure. Mum booked a private walk with a local geology expert in a place further along the coast called Lyme Regis. It's a well-known area on the Jurassic Coast, and they have a small museum and shop with lots of fossils. I understand you've been asking questions about the past. You can help carry everything we need to the car."

They finished breakfast, brushed their teeth, and packed the car. Then they all piled in, eager for the trip.

"Tell us more about this place, Mum," said Will.

"It was made famous because a lady called Mary Anning found the first dinosaur bones on the coast there. So many people know about it now that it's impossible to find any more dinosaur bones, but we may find some fossils. It can get very crowded, so I booked this private walk with the resident geologist. He can take us to parts of the beach least visited."

"It will be fairly early in the day and shouldn't be too crowded yet. The scenery on the way is very pretty, and you can see along the coastline," Dad added. "If you look at one of the maps we brought, you can see the route and its extent."

Will was looking out of the window. "Look over there. You can see the coast for miles and miles."

They continued the drive, looking out at a very long, pebbly beach, stretching far into the distance. When they reached Lyme Regis, they parked in a lot on top of the hill. Collecting their backpacks, they walked down into the town.

Entering the shop that doubled as a museum, they met the geologist in charge.

"Good morning to you all. My name is Robert, and I'll be taking you for our walk this morning. We'll be leaving in a few minutes so have a look around our small museum while you wait."

"Mum, I know you have a hammer, but can we buy another one between us please?" asked Pete.

"Yes, you can buy it while we're waiting but don't take too long. We can have a good look around when we've finished the walk."

The hammer bought, they followed Robert out of the shop and down the hill. Following their guide along the promenade, they gazed at the sea as they walked to a pebbly beach.

"We're going to walk quite a bit farther on, because everybody starts looking for fossils as soon as they hit the beach. As we go, I'll point out some very large ammonites to you, which of course we shall not be picking up!" He shook his finger at them playfully and laughed.

Indeed, there were large, curly snail-like stones, and even though they had been considerably worn through the pounding of the sea, the tell-tale shapes were still visible.

"Don't go too close to the cliffs. They can be slippery, especially after a storm." Bending down, Robert picked up a flattish rock. "Tap the edge with your hammer and break it open."

"Oh look!" said Will. "There's a snail-like shape embedded on the inside."

"Lucky you," said Robert. "That's a fossil, and you're lucky to find one. It's difficult to find any decent sized ones these days."

Will beamed in delight at his find, but the others weren't so lucky.

"I'll share it with you, if you want to borrow it for school," Will told his brothers.

Robert said, "Pour a little seawater on it, and you'll be able to see it more clearly."

After a lot more searching, the others eventually found one very small fossil each.

"Mr. Robert, has anyone ever found any fossils of animals which may have had wings as well as four legs? I know about pterodactyls and other flying dinosaurs, but could any of them have walked on the ground with four feet as well?" Nat asked.

"Ah, I know what you've been reading: books about dragons. I'm sorry to disappoint you, but nobody has ever found the bones of a creature that could have developed into a dragon. They are purely mythical. You see, to develop into a dragon, there would have to have been creatures with six limbs adjoining the spine. Then two may have developed into shoulders and wings with the other four becoming front and back legs. The only creatures with more than four legs are creatures like insects which do not have the same skeletal structure at all."

"What about bats?" Will asked.

"No, once again, sorry. They only have the same four limb structure. It's a pity, as I too, when I was young, longed to find some proof of the existence of dragons."

For one moment, Nat thought how great it would be to tell Robert of their discovery but realized the adult would never believe it.

They walked on slowly, looking around all the time, but even though they tried many hopeful looking rocks, they didn't find more fossils. Asking many questions about the rock formations locally, they were back at the museum shop all too soon. After thanking Robert for guiding them, they looked around the shop.

"I wonder if Brecky has ever—ouch. You stepped on me, Pete," complained Nat.

"Who's Brecky? What an unusual name," said Mum.

"Oh, just a girl we met on the beach."

"That's nice. Boys, would you mind if Dad and I went off on our own and looked at some of the other shops?"

"Of course not," Pete said.

"Do you remember passing a restaurant on the way down to the beach front?"

"Yes," said Nat.

"Meet us at that restaurant for lunch."

"That sounds good."

After they had agreed on a time to meet, the boys began looking in earnest for a souvenir. There were so many interesting things, but in the end, they decided to buy small fossils for themselves and for the girls.

Will picked up a large colored poster. "It's a picture of the coastline around here and its changes over the millions of years. We could show the girls what happened to our world in the distant past. It'd be a lot easier than just talking about it."

Nat pointed out some books. "Right. And here's one with illustrations showing how fossils formed."

"We might even be able to get them to look for fossils in their world," added Will.

They chose a few things they thought might help them explain the earth's past.

Pete found maps. "I wonder if Brecky has the ones her father found or if he took them with him. Let's ask her to take us to the spot where he found them."

"If we're finished here, let's pay for our stuff. I hope we haven't spent too much. We've still got several weeks to go!" exclaimed Nat.

After paying, they made their way down the hill to meet their parents at the restaurant. They were enjoying lunch when their mother noticed their packages.

"You must have nearly cleared the shop out!" Mum said.

"Those look like young children's books. Aren't you a bit old for them?" asked Dad.

"Yes," agreed Pete, "but the illustrations are so clear. I'd like to study more, but the bigger books were too expensive."

As they walked to the car, Nat waited until their parents were lagging behind. "I wonder if there are any fossils near where the girls live and if Jessynta can tell us more about ancient creatures."

"I would have thought all the upheavals they say occurred would have unearthed something. Maybe we could get the dragons to dig around. The books we bought should show them what we mean by fossils," said Pete. "Careful! Here come Mum and Dad."

"There's definitely a lot to do around this part of the country. I'm glad you brought us here," said Nat. "I don't think I'll miss my screen time at all, and I know we won't get bored."

"I'm glad to hear that," replied Mum with a suspicious glance at them.

"Much better than spending a lot of time on your screens anyway. It's good to see you so enthusiastic about everything you've seen. I hope you don't feel like you missed out on a more active vacation," Dad said.

Will's face broke into a satisfied smirk.

"What's so funny?" she asked.

"It's nothing. Just a private joke," Pete rushed to cover his brother's slip. "We're having fun."

When they reached home, they went straight upstairs. Pete punched Will's arm. "You nearly let the cat out of the bag again, Will. This is getting impossible."

"Let's go to Avalanya now," pleaded Nat. "It's not dark yet, and I'm still worried about Edwith."

Pete hesitated. "It might be night there. We should wait until tomorrow."

Nat said angrily, "Why are you always trying to spoil things for me? You're not our mother."

"I am older than you, though."

"Ha, by one hour, if that."

"Oh come on, you two. Let's not ruin our day with an argument," Will said.

"Boys, you're making a lot of noise and Dad's online with his office. Can't you go read or something," Mum called from downstairs.

Nat whispered, "Can we try the shells again?"

Pete placed his backpack with the shells on his bed.

"No, they are limited use. We need to just wait until tomorrow."

CHAPTER SEVEN

"NAT, AREN'T YOU UP a little early?" said Pete when his brother woke him.

"Not really, I'm eager to see Edwith. He was so upset when we left. Hurry up! Will and I have already eaten breakfast."

Rubbing his eyes, Pete got out of bed, washed, dressed, and went down to the kitchen. Their mother walked in the front door. "Hi, Mum! Where have you been?"

"The office needed Dad for some urgent meetings today, so I took him to the station. He may be away for a couple of days again. It's really annoying. He was looking forward to spending more time with us. Hopefully after this, he'll be able to take a longer break. I have a few things to do today, so you can go off by yourselves if you don't mind me not coming with you."

"Of course. Don't worry, we have our phones. We have plenty to keep us busy," said Nat, smirking.

She looked at them suspiciously but didn't say anything.

Stuffing a slice of toast in his mouth, Pete rushed back to his bedroom to pack the things they had bought the day before in a backpack. The other two followed.

Nat added a tin of prettily wrapped chocolate. "I think the girls might like these."

Chattering excitedly, they rushed to the cave.

Quickly, they pulled aside the fronds and climbed down the rope.

"Look! Jessynta's nest area has been cleared out," said Nat.

They exited the cave. "The entrance is bigger, and the way onto the beach has been cleared. The rubble is gone," Will said.

Pete gasped in surprise when he saw the two dragons. "Wow! We've only been away two days but look at the size of you both."

Nat gazed at Edwith. "You must be as big as a pony now and almost as large as Jessynta."

Both dragons bounded over to the three boys as fast as they could. Edwith nearly knocked Nat over in his exuberance.

We have grown some. We do not know how big we will get. Hopefully quite a lot bigger than now, as we are supposed to grow for several months and sometimes as long as half a year. We do our growing at night while asleep, but our scales get a little itchy. The girls have been rubbing oil into our skin to help, but bits do tend to flake off, said Jessynta.

I am a male dragon. I shall end up larger than Jessynta.

You hope! But I admit you most likely will. Better take care your head does not get too big, or you might overbalance!

Everyone laughed at that, even Edwith.

"I'm so relieved to see you, Edwith. I've been having such awful dreams, and I thought you must be in trouble." Nat stroked the delighted dragon's nose.

Brecky admitted, "We did have trouble getting him settled, because he was really upset when we had to leave as well."

Edwith hung his head. *I had only just been born and when you three boys left, I felt so lonely. Then when Izchettya said she could not stay with me in the cave either, it was awful. I thought the idea of having two bond mates was so we would not have to be alone.*

"We found a lovely big cave for him, but he didn't want to be by himself, but he wouldn't share with Jessynta either," said Izzy. "Luckily, Lanya had an idea."

"We have several stables on the farm. We used nice, clean,

new straw to made a bed for him there. We found blankets and made beds for ourselves. Then Jessynta came too."

There was no way I would let him sleep out of my sight. He could get up to mischief.

As if I would, said Edwith indignantly. *I have turned over a new tree.*

Everyone burst out laughing.

"You mean, 'I have turned over a new leaf,'" said Izzy.

Whatever. I really am going to try hard to stay out of trouble. I promise.

"Anyway, he did behave, although it was a struggle getting him settled down, and our mother wasn't too keen on us sleeping in the stables with the dragons, but after she had met Jessynta and had a long talk with her, she agreed."

Nat's eyes opened wide. "Your mother met them?"

Yes, a lovely lady she is too. Jessynta gazed into the distance. *I wish I had met my mother. I quite envy you having a mother around as you grow up. When I told her that, she said she would adopt me. Instead of using her formal name, I am to call her Mother Skyla. She gave us a nice apple drink. I really think she trusts us and will not worry too much when we are strong enough to carry people.*

"What? Wait a minute! Do you mean we're going to fly with you up in the sky?" Nat's mouth fell open in shock.

Jessynta spread her wings to demonstrate. *Of course. We are dragons, and that is why we have wings. Not for a while yet though.*

I am not sure how Jessynta will carry anyone with her shorter wings, Edwith said.

They all looked more closely at Jessynta. Now that she had grown bigger, they could see that her wings were indeed a lot shorter than Edwith's.

Take no notice of Edwith. I will be able to carry you in the air, but I will do a great deal of swimming as well. I have magical abilities that will enable me to move through the air as if it were water. It should be instinctive once I am strong enough to try. Already, if I walk fast, I begin to rise a little.

Opening his eyes wide in surprise, Nat pointed to her wings. "Ooh, look she's rotating them. They look like fins."

"Those strange frills on her sides are waving up and down like ripples." Will pointed to the dragon. "And what about that huge tail? It looks like a whale's."

I, too, will rely on instinct, but as you know, I am going to be the biggest dragon that ever lived. You will see. Edwith puffed himself up.

Show off! Jessynta stretched herself out to a truly impressive length.

The children were highly amused at this display of one-upmanship on the part of the two dragons.

Will was about to comment, when Brecky said, "You shouldn't let them boast to you, especially Edwith. He's like this all the time."

They cannot have failed to notice how magnificent I am. Look how my scales change colors as I turn around. He spun around, waving his wings in the sun. Unfortunately, he tripped over his rather long tail and fell on his snout. *Ouch!*

They all laughed except Nat and Izzy, who both ran over to make sure he hadn't really hurt himself.

Jessynta added, *You had better learn to get more control over that ungainly body of yours, even though you are rather a magnificent specimen of dragonhood. Remember, you only just hatched, and it will take time to get your balance.*

It is easy for you to say, as you are lower to the ground.

"Never mind, Edwith. You must be more careful and take it slower," said Nat. "Sorry we laughed at you."

The ever-incorrigible Edwith joined in the laughter. *Perhaps I could take up tumbling and entertain you all. I do have to grow a lot larger if you are going to ride on my back.*

"Is that going to happen soon?" asked Izzy. "We had better begin making saddles. We'll have to adapt some horse saddles and that will take some thought. Lanya is really good at working with leather."

"I'll need a lot of help, because they'll have to be bigger and still leave room for growth." Lanya frowned in concentration as she looked the two dragons up and down.

Now for our caves. You may have noticed that my cave is empty. While we were looking for a cave to suit Edwith, I found one that I really loved for myself. My original cave was quite small. So I decided to move. Come along and I will show you my new home.

And do not forget mine. I found the largest one in the cliff, and it is super. I have not actually slept there yet. The girls' mother is organizing men to bring us loads of hay to make them comfortable.

Noise sounded from the cliff pathway as four men pushed carts loaded with hay down to the beach.

"Show us where you want this, Master Edwith and Madam Jessynta," said one of the men.

Right over here. Some in this first cave and some in that one over there. Thank you, gentlemen, said Jessynta.

Pete looked surprised. "They know your names. How can they hear you? And what's this master and madam business?"

Brecky giggled. "Jessynta told them that she, as a queen, should be addressed more regally, so they decided to call her madam."

I discovered in a memory that I can talk to anyone if I really need to. For special occasions I use a group voice.

Hey, young Marek, I am a very big dragon, so please make sure you give me the biggest load of hay, said Edwith.

"Of course, Master Edwith. I understand. You are rather large." He grinned broadly and unloaded the hay into the appropriate caves, assisted by Edwith.

Oh, not on top of me, said Edwith from under a massive pile of hay.

What do you expect? You had better keep out of their way, said Jessynta.

"Miss Brecky, your mother told me you needed a sturdy ladder at the rear of that cave over there." Marek pointed to the cave the boys had come from.

"Yes, Marek. You will see there's a long rope tied to the wall at the back. Please anchor the ladder where the rope emerges."

"Okay, Miss Brecky. Erico and I will measure it and try to think of something. Your mother swore us to secrecy about this project, and it's more than our life is worth to disobey her."

Pete looked at his brothers. "That does sound like a great idea. To tell the truth, I was a little worried about our mother coming here if she had to come down using our rope."

The other men continued loading hay into the dragons' caves, until finally, even Edwith announced he was happy with his new home.

Marek and Erico came out of the cave, and all the workers left.

Brecky returned to one of their much earlier questions about timekeeping. "We don't need absolute accuracy most of the time, but we do use a timing method for cooking meals, work on the farm, and chores. We'll show you when you visit our house. However, when we're out, we cannot use it, as it isn't easy to carry around."

"Actually," continued Lanya, "our father was working on something portable he called a time-teller with his brother Aleto, Ven's father, who loves to invent things. They were excavating ruins and unearthed old iron chests in a pit in the ground. Unfortunately, when they opened them, a lot of the material rotted away. He did save some bits, and Uncle Aleto is busy using them to finish the time-teller.

"Where is Ven today?" asked Pete. "I'd like to talk to him

again and see what he and his father are storing."

"He lives on the other side of the estuary. It's quite a walk, so he doesn't come every day. But we can walk over there another time."

"That sounds good." Pete opened his backpack. "Look at what we bought for you yesterday."

"Pretty pictures, but what are those black squiggles? We don't have material like this. What is it?" asked Brecky, holding the book.

"Those are pictures of things in our world, and the squiggles are our written language. Don't you have books?"

"We had animal skins with our old written language, and although our father could understand it, not many others can anymore."

Lanya was looking at the poster. "Is this what your world looks like?"

"No. It's what it used to look like thousands and thousands of years ago."

"What are these?" Brecky picked up the shiny rocks that had fallen onto the sand.

Shiny rocks! said Jessynta trotting over. *Come and look at these shiny rocks, Edwith. See how they sparkle in the sun?*

"We brought them for you," said Nat.

I will take them to decorate my cave, said Edwith, trying to clasp one in his claws.

Jessynta poked him with her paw. *You may not have them all. We must share.* She asked the boys, *How did they get so shiny?*

"If you rub some of the rocks on your beach very hard, they will shine too." Will showed her, using the edge of his shirt.

These things look a bit like creatures carved into pieces of rock, said Edwith, pawing a fossil.

"Millions and millions of years ago, these little creatures swam around in the ocean. After lots of earth and rocks covered them over, they turned into stone. We call them fossils. Don't you have them?" asked Will.

"I've never seen things like them," said Izzy.

Will opened the tin. "Try these. They taste really good." He showed them how to take off the wrappers and eat the chocolate inside.

"They do taste good. Try one, Jessynta." Brecky offered one to the dragon, but it was so tiny, she wasn't interested.

The dragons were more interested in the colored, shiny foil they were wrapped in. They were absolutely delighted when the girls wrapped each piece around a small pebble.

Ooh, I like them. Could you get me more please? asked Edwith.

"Okay, but there isn't much left. As you like the paper so much, I'll look for more like it at home," said Pete.

Looking at the dragons pawing the pebbles, Brecky said, "Let's leave them to it, and we'll take you to meet our mother."

"She knows about us as well as the dragons?" asked Nat. "We haven't told our mother yet."

"Yes, and she remembers folktales about dragons from when she was a little girl. She always wished she could have met one, so we introduced her to them. When we told her about you three, she was really amazed. She's longing to meet you."

I do like her so much, said Jessynta rather wistfully. *We will stay here and finish getting our new homes arranged and sort our new decorations. We cannot stay in your stables much longer. I do not believe your horses were too keen on us being so near them.*

I know not to eat them now.

Yes, but they do not know that. It will take quite a while for them to get used to our smell.

I do not smell! Edwith stamped his foot.

But you do to them, and they smell too. Do they not, children? All animals smell of something.

If you say so. When you go up to your farm, I could manage a few more snacks.

Edwith, I was serious about you overeating. If you eat too much, you won't be able to fly. Your stomach might burst if you carry on eating at this rate.

Not so, I am going to be a very big dragon, so I must eat a lot of food until I am fully grown. However, maybe instead, I will sit in the sun and rest. Perhaps you could bring more of that nice creamy stuff and rub in more when you come back, please?

The children couldn't help laughing at the dragons' conversation. "Enjoy your rest. Don't let your scales dry out too much. We'll be sure to bring back some of the ointment," said Brecky.

We will both smell really nice and maybe the horses will even like us then, said Edwith.

CHAPTER EIGHT

THE BOYS WERE EXCITED to see where the girls lived.

When they saw it, Will couldn't help remarking, "It looks a little like the pictures of medieval buildings with walls of stone and flint. I expected it to look very different from our world's houses."

Nat stared hard at the smaller buildings. "The outbuildings are made of stone and wood and have slate tiles on their roofs."

Stables with horses and ponies peering over the doors stood on the side of the farmyard. "Lovely horses. Lots of them too." Pete pointed to the side of the field. "And a real working watermill."

Surprised, Izzy said. "Don't you have watermills in your world?"

"Yes, we do but not many are working anymore."

"Where does your flour come from?"

"We buy it from our shops."

Izzy opened her mouth to speak, but a tall, dark-haired woman who looked like a slightly older Brecky came out of the door. "Brecky, bring the boys. I want to meet them."

"Mother, meet Pete, Nat, and Will."

"So, these are the other-world travelers who have turned my life upside down. Pleased to meet you all. Call me Skyla."

"Good to meet you," Pete said. "Sorry if we've made life

hard for you. Maybe we could make it up to you by helping find your husband."

"When our dragons are old enough to fly," Nat added.

"I don't see how. Brin has been gone for a very long time now but thanks for the offer." Skyla wiped her hands on a dish towel. "I don't know when you last had food, but you are welcome to share our meal. Come in and make yourselves at home. Girls, why don't you show the boys around the house?"

"Don't go any trouble for us." Pete smiled at her politely.

"No trouble at all. My girls are always hungry, and we grow most of our food right here."

The girls proudly showed them their house. "This is our main room." Brecky led the way through a very large wooden door. "We do most everything in here. We cook on the fire, and it heats the brick oven next to it."

Will looked around. "We don't use a fire to cook on, but I remember seeing rooms like this in some of the old houses we've been to in England."

Lanya looked at her sisters' curious expressions and spoke for them all. "How do you cook then?"

"On stoves and other gadgets for the kitchen. We live a very different life in our world."

"You must." Lanya gestured to a door on the left. "That's where our parents sleep."

"Where do you sleep?" asked Will.

"On the right side. Follow me."

Following her up a very sturdy set of steep wooden stairs, they came to a balcony topped with branches that crossed the length of the floor. The large area was divided into three separate rooms with beds.

Nat studied the beams on the ceiling. "Look at that, Will. It's like the one we have in our rental cottage, but ours doesn't have all those twigs and things tied around it."

"The ropes keep the thatch in place," said Lanya. "Mother

is a healer, and those are plants she uses. We hang them to dry indoors."

"I don't think I've ever seen so many." Nat touched the twigs on the cupboards and windowsills.

Brecky laughed. "I sometimes wonder if our house isn't just a place for her to keep her plants."

"Where's the bathroom?"

"What's a bath room?" Brecky pronounced it like two words.

"Where we wash ourselves."

"Oh, we have a room at the back of the house that our father fixed up as a place for us to wash. Next to that is the outhouse."

"Thanks to our father, who tapped into the hot springs outside and put in a pump and pipes, we have lots of water available to run water into the house," said Lanya. "The area around here has many underground hot springs, and there are loads of old, hollow pipes lying around. From the ancient people, no doubt."

"Even though they're old, with a few repairs, they work," Izzy said.

"Dad told us that ages and ages ago, there must have been some volcanoes nearby, so there's a lot of hot water underground if you know where to look for it," added Brecky.

"Food's on the table. Come and eat," called Skyla.

They sat down at a long table to a fantastic spread. Some food they recognized from picnics with the girls.

"Ooh, taste these yummy, hard-boiled eggs. The yolks are bright orange." Will stuffed his face. "Scrumptious cake with lashings of cream. Do you eat like this every day?"

"It all depends on what we have around."

"That was smashing. Thanks so much, Miss Skyla." Nat scraped his plate clean. "Can we help you clean up?"

"No. Leave everything on the table. One of the farm workers' wives helps me if I need it. Let my girls show you the rest of the farm."

"Come on then, hurry up." Izzy ran outside. Chasing after her, they ran to a barn behind the house, crammed with all sorts of things.

"Here are some of the things Father found. He took some with him, and Uncle Aleto is looking after some," said Brecky. "Father was told there was once a large city further north on the mainland. He wanted to explore it with his best friend."

"In spite of being warned about possible dangers, he had to go north." Lanya huffed out a breath. "The only people who come here to trade come from the south."

"Our mother can scry, so she was able to see him several times during his journey, but not long after he landed on the mainland, she lost complete trace of him. We don't know why," said Izzy.

"We don't do scrying in our world," said Will.

"How do you know where people are and what they're doing?" asked Izzy.

"We have computers and portable devices called smart phones. We can talk to and see people on them, but it isn't magic. You just buy the devices and push buttons." Nat mimed dialing a phone in his hand.

"Sounds like magic to me." Brecky shrugged. "Why don't we see how the dragons are?"

They stopped to say goodbye to Skyla at the house and thanked her again for lunch.

Skyla put away what she was working on. "I'll come with you. I love those darling dragons. Let me get some of the ointment they like."

When they reached the bottom of the cliff steps, Jessynta and Edwith were waiting for them.

I heard a faint call in my head and wondered if any of you had heard it too, said Jessynta.

"I didn't hear anything," said Nat.

I am not sure, as it is very faint. Edwith did not hear it. It appears to be coming from a long way. Maybe behind your farm. Do you know what land is up there?

"Only mountains and an extinct volcano called Solfarania. I know it well," said Skyla. "I sometimes go there with my sister Suki and other healers. There are many hot caves around its rim, and it smells a bit horrible like rotten eggs. The heat makes people sweat, and it clears the lungs. We take people with breathing problems there for short visits, and it seems to help them."

"Let's go check it out," said Nat.

Skyla frowned. "It's no longer active, but it's still dangerous with only a thin crust over the top of the volcano. You'll need to be very careful. The crust is fragile in some areas. If you get too close, the crust could give way, and you'd fall into a muddy, bubbling, extremely hot pool. We roped off the very thin areas and never ever go into the middle.

"Volcano, bubbling mud? How could another dragon egg be there? Doesn't sound possible," Pete said.

On the contrary, said Jessynta. *It sounds like it could be a fire dragon egg. Their mothers usually lay them near heat.*

"Off on another search then? Can we go now? Maybe my turn to bond with a dragon has come." Will clapped his hands in delight.

"Not so fast, young Will. Definitely not enough time to go and come back today. We need time to get ready, and it's too far to walk." Seeing his face fall, Skyla continued. "I guess we could use the horse and cart. I could drive it. Jessynta and Edwith could ride in it. The rest of you can ride ponies."

"We haven't ridden except for odd pony rides," said Will.

"It's easy. We have really gentle ponies," said Izzy. "We won't go fast. Mother teaches riding to the villagers, so she'll show you."

"Of course. No problem, boys." Skyla smiled reassuringly.

"I've always wanted to learn to ride." Will was all smiles

again. "Jessynta, do you think the dragon will be all right if it's a little longer before we can reach it? Will it hatch before we get there?"

Do not worry about that. We sense a possible bond partner is near before we begin hatching. I can reassure it that help is on its way. In any case, it has not actually called to you yet.

"The cart will be pretty crowded if three dragons are in it," said Will.

"The one we use to transport hay and animals to market is quite large. Though we might have to put Edwith on a diet tomorrow," said Brecky.

Edwith howled. *Oh no! I shall starve and turn into a skeleton. My stomach is already starting to hurt with the very thought of it. You would not, would you? You do not mean it, do you?*

"You really mustn't tease the poor creature," said Skyla. "They are just teasing you, Edwith. I've a good mind to send them to bed tonight without any dinner."

I will eat theirs for them then!

Enough! said Jessynta. *This is unnecessary. There will not be three of us. Where does the river that runs your watermill come from? If it starts close to the volcano, I can swim instead of riding in your cart. That is best for me.*

"The river starts from the edge of the mountain close to the volcano, then continues down to join another river just before the estuary, so you should be able to swim up from the sea," replied Skyla.

"That sounds great. It'll leave more room in the cart if the new dragon is large. Newly hatched dragons are very hungry, so we'd better take food with us," said Pete.

There had better be a lot of food because I might get a little hungry on the way. Of course, a lot of the food will get eaten before we return, so we will not be too crowded. If our new dragon is as hungry as I, we must make sure to have lots and lots.

"As if we could ever forget you need a lot of food, but you mustn't be greedy," said Izzy with a laugh. "We'll bring our bows and arrows and might even find some wild game as we travel. We can begin collecting things we might need for the journey today. How long do you think it will take us, Mother?"

"I don't really know. It might take us some time to search the area, in addition to the three leagues to get there."

Will spoke very quickly. "That's probably nine to ten of our miles. I know because I read some books about old English measurements—supposing that Avalanya's leagues are the same."

"Our horses met the dragons when they slept in the stables, but we still need to be careful with them. Horses get spooked easily. We'll have to get them used to being so close to the dragons gradually," said Brecky.

Meanwhile, Edwith was showing off, lifting himself off the ground by jumping and flapping his wings.

I learn fast, do I not? he asked, promptly falling on his snout.

"If you can play around like that, there really is no reason why you can't walk behind the horses. It's a long way though. We'll have to see tomorrow," said Skyla.

Oh no, I am not sure about that. I am not designed to walk far yet.

Pete looked at the sky. "It's been fun, but it's time for us to go home. However, we'll try to do some shell talk to shorten the time."

"How much time do you think has gone by here?" asked Nat.

Brecky looked at where the sun was. "From the position of the sun in the sky, it's late in the afternoon."

"We've done a lot here; it must be at least the equivalent of a day in our world. We'll see when we return how much time has gone by there," said Pete. "Jessynta, I nearly forgot to ask you. Can we have one of your scales to show our mother?

She'll have to believe us when she sees it. I vote we tell her everything tonight."

Jessynta gently eased off one of the scales from under her front leg. It looked painful, but she assured them that it happened all the time as she grew.

Pete held the slightly curved scale up to the light. It was the size of a small clam shell but flatter. "See how it shines when the sun hits it? It looks like a small abalone shell, but the colors are like sea water. Mum is going to love this."

"Do you think we could bring her here, Jessynta?" asked Nat.

I do not see why not.

"Miss Skyla, if she comes with us, can we take her with us to look for the dragon egg?"

"Certainly. We have plenty of horses, and I'd like to meet her."

"I'm glad we're going to tell her. I feel bad about sneaking off without telling Mum where we're going," said Nat.

"And now she'll understand why we all have such enormous appetites," said Will. "I can't wait to see her face when she meets Jessynta and Edwith."

Edwith, give them one of your scales too.

He looked around his body. When he gave a little shake, a scale came loose.

Nat picked it up and held it like he had seen Pete do. "Wait 'til she sees this one. The green is transparent like the waves get when they're just about to break."

Will looked at his older brother in admiration. "That sounds like you've been reading poetry."

Nat gave him a playful shove. "She has to see that these are no ordinary scales, and we can also show her the shell pieces."

The boys took the scales and went back to the cave. The way up the rope seemed easier every time they tried it. However, Pete hoped the workmen would have the stairs finished soon.

Their mother was looking a little anxious by the time they got home. "I was wondering where you all were. I even walked to the end of the garden and called you, but there was no answer."

"Aah," said Pete grinning from ear to ear. "That was because we were not actually in this world at all!"

"Ha-ha, there you go again. You've been reading too many fantasy books."

"Let's sit down, and we'll tell you something really fantastic."

CHAPTER NINE

THE BOYS GATHERED IN the living room with their mother.

"I wasn't ill at all," Pete said. "A voice in my head made me want to go into the woods. I didn't know what was happening. I finally persuaded Nat and Will to come with me, and I fell down a tunnel into a cave."

"He completely disappeared, and then I heard him shout," said Nat.

"Pete, hurry up and tell her the rest of it. She doesn't need to have all the details." Will grabbed her hand. "We followed him and guess what! We all ended up in another world and helped a dragon hatch."

Their mother burst out laughing. "That's a roundabout way to describe a new game you want to play. Am I supposed to play it with you? I hope you don't expect me to climb down tunnels in the woods."

"No, it's not a game. We really did end up in another universe," said Will.

Nat jumped in. "It's called Avalanya."

"We found an egg. I touched the shell while we were helping it hatch, and I felt a little burn on my hand." Pete held his hand up for his mother's inspection. "Look at the mark. It's faded a bit and it's very small. Look closely. Nat has one too, exactly the same."

Nat held up his hand too. "That's just a freckle," she said.

"Look again. They're identically shaped," said Nat. "What are the chances of that?"

When she still didn't look impressed, Pete produced items from his backpack. "Take a look at this! It's a piece of the dragon's eggshell, and *this* is a dragon scale."

"Here's *my* dragon's green scale and a piece of his shell." Nat didn't want to be overshadowed.

Their mother took the pieces and studied them closely. "They are beautiful and unlike anything I've seen. Wait a minute." She went to her room and returned with her geologist's magnifying eyepiece.

The boys watched her reactions eagerly, fidgeting impatiently.

She frowned as studied them, turning them over and over in her hands. "I must say, these are unusual looking artifacts and such pretty colors. I'd like to see where you found them. However, these are not enough to convince me that what you have said is true, even though I've never known you to lie. Perhaps there's something in your outlandish tale. Though mind you, I'm not convinced yet."

While she was peering at the objects, they told her about meeting the girls on the beach.

"So you did meet a girl named Brecky?"

"We did, but the girls don't speak our language, so we couldn't understand each other. It's crazy but true. You have to put your hands on somebody's head, and they imprint their language to your brain. When you talk to them, they can understand you! They call it a mind meld." Will beamed with pride at his explanation.

Their mother threw her hands up in despair. "This is all too much to take in. Are you sure you're not playing some game? It's a good thing Dad's not here. He'd be laughing his head off."

"Wait until you see Jessynta. That's the dragon's name.

She's so beautiful, and although she can't speak our language, she speaks directly into our heads," Pete said.

Will sat up straight, showing off his knowledge. "Telepathy!"

"Oh no! Is there more?" she asked.

"Yes. A few days later, another dragon hatched. His name's Edwith, and the green shell piece is his. Oh, Mum, you'll just love him. He's an absolute clown. He's always tripping up, and he gets words mixed up, and I can't wait for you to meet him." Nat was babbling in his excitement. He stopped to take a deep breath.

"I haven't had a dragon call me yet but might meet one soon. One's ready to hatch, and we want you to come with us," added Will.

"What am I going to do with you all?" She put her hands to her head and shook it from side to side in disbelief.

"Slow down, Nat. Mum's getting confused with your chattering." Pete focused his attention on his mother. "Mum, this is important. There seems to be another dragon ready to hatch, and we're all going in search tomorrow. Like Will said, we want you to come with us and see for yourself.

"What else are you going to come up with? This is quite an unbelievable tale!"

"No, don't shake your head again. It's on the edge of a mountain near where they live. It's too far to walk, so we're riding. They have horses. Mum, can you ride?" Will asked.

"Yes, I can ride, but it's been ages. Where are you getting horses?"

"All arranged. The girls have horses. They live on a farm," Pete said.

"So come with us tomorrow. You might want to bring your special hammer too. With your knowledge of geology, you might find some clues." Nat grinned broadly.

"I must say, you sound very convincing with a well-rehearsed tale, but I still don't believe it."

"Make sure you wear comfortable clothes. We always end up climbing around a bit," said Pete.

She laughed. "I knew it! A game!"

"Don't laugh. You won't regret it," he added.

By this time, the boys were all talking at once. Their mother slumped in her seat. "I need a rest. You're all chattering so fast, I can hardly understand you."

She closed her eyes and put her head in her hands again. Finally, she shrugged her shoulders in resignation. "Seeing as how Dad's still away and not likely to be back for several days, I might as well come with you and 'play' your game."

Pete continued, "You may have some ideas to help us. There are more dragons to be found. As far as we can tell from conversations with Jessynta, Avalanya has to be an alternate universe where people lived in huge cities thousands of years ago. The ancient people who lived there almost destroyed it with wars, disease, and pollution, causing climate change like the scientists keep warning us about."

"You can't be serious!" She sighed. "I'll have to sleep on it, and we'll see tomorrow."

"Do you mind if we go for a short walk now? It's still light out."

"All right, and I'll have a word with Dad about your latest antics." She stood and walked out of the room.

"Oh goodness, I hope he won't dissuade her," said Will as they left the house.

"Let's take the shells to the top of the garden to talk to the dragons. We can get chairs out of the shed."

Jessynta was the first dragon to start the conversation.

Did you talk to your mother? What did she say? Can you hear me all right, William?

"Yes, I can hear you clearly," said Will.

"We told her," said Pete, "but she didn't believe a word of it. She thought we were making it all up. She was very surprised at the scales and shell pieces though, so maybe she'll at least come out of curiosity. What have you been up to?"

We have been busy since you left, decorating our new caves with shells and pretty fronds of seaweed. You will be very surprised when you see it, said Jessynta.

"We're worried about our mother climbing into the cave in the dark," said Nat.

Do not worry about that. We have made some changes. Wait until you s—

Edwith, stop! Do not dare tell them! You will spoil the surprise.

"Edwith, you sound happy, and you've really got the hang of this shell speaking. Is Izzy taking care of you and feeding you well?" asked Nat anxiously.

She is stuffing me full of lots of nice, tasty meat.

Mother Skyla has made soothing ointment for our itches, and the girls help to rub it in. We really love her. She is looking forward to meeting your mother. We are too.

Ooh yes, and I shall be on my very best behavior. I have been extra good.

You are certainly trying harder anyway.

"Jessynta, have you heard any more from the dragon who was calling you?" Will asked.

Yes, its voice is a little clearer, but I do not know any more about it or who it will bond with but keep your claws—I mean fingers—crossed!

"It's beginning to get a little dark here, so we should stop," said Pete. "Jessynta, you said that talking to you with the shells might help to make our time closer. I hope it works."

I hope so too. Her voice faded out.

"Mum better come with us tomorrow," said Nat as they put away the shells and made their way home.

"She was intrigued with the shells. We'll have to be extremely persuasive tomorrow morning," Pete said.

"Being able to talk to the dragons was great. I wonder what their surprise will be," said Will.

~~~~~

The sun was shining brightly the next morning when the boys rushed down the stairs to eat breakfast.

"It's such a lovely day. Are you sure you want to go into dark old woods instead of the beach?" Mum asked.

Their faces fell. "But, Mum, you *must* come. Didn't our talk last night make you curious? Or do you still doubt us?" asked Nat.

"The pieces you showed me are a bit of a mystery, so I suppose I had better come to see where you got them. The shell pieces resemble fossil shells but have one or two anomalies. I would need quite sophisticated means to test them completely. As for the pieces of what you say are cast-off dragon scales, they are truly amazing, although they do look a bit like abalone shells."

"You won't regret it," said Pete. "Don't forget your hammer, and dress like we told you for a little climbing. Don't make a face. It really is true. You'll see."

Breakfast over and cleared away, Pete eagerly led the way up the hill. As they neared the cave where their rope was tied, Pete pointed at the tree.

"See that rope, Mum? It goes right under that huge rock. Now how do you think that happened?"
~~~~~

CHAPTER TEN

Welcome to all of you.

The boys were extremely surprised to hear her voice in their heads.

"We're not even inside yet," said Pete. "This never happened before."

As they pushed the fronds aside, the rock disappeared.

Rachel looked bewildered. "Where did the rock go? Where did the beautiful lights come from?"

Looking into the cave, they were able to see it as never before. Small globes full of water and a phosphorescent glow lined the cave walls.

"Oh, how beautiful," exclaimed their mother in surprise. "How did you do this?"

"We didn't," confessed Pete, as he moved forward. "We're just as surprised as you. We've seen the lights before, because Jessynta used some to decorate her cave. She must have decided to use them to light our way. And look, there are now stairs with handrails. We used to have to climb down holding onto a rope, and we were concerned about how you would manage. Brecky said their workmen would make this, but I didn't know when it would be ready."

They carefully climbed down the new stairway. At the foot, two gleaming dragons awaited them. Their mother took a step backward, so stunned by the sight of them that she couldn't say a word. She dumbly followed the boys and dragons outside.

Pete turned back to her. "You see, Mum, we told you the truth, and this is only the beginning. Just look at the sea and sky and tell me if there is any way this could be our earth!"

Still stunned, she looked around her and spotted Skyla and her daughters standing nearby. Before she could ask who they were, Jessynta bent her head down to Rachel's level.

Please ask your mother to touch me and give me permission to speak with her.

"We told you how we touched the dragons so they could communicate telepathically. First touch Jessynta, as she is the queen. I promise you they aren't the least bit dangerous," said Pete.

A little reluctantly, Rachel stepped forward. With trembling hands, she reached out to Jessynta, who bowed her huge head solemnly in front of her.

A very great welcome to you, Most Revered Lady Mother Rachel. We are so happy to receive you in our land of Avalanya. We have awaited the meeting of our two worlds since it was foretold by our ancestors that humans would come to help us. And indeed, your sons have begun this task extremely well. You are to be congratulated on having such fine, intelligent and willing boys. They do you and their father credit.

Rachel clapped her hands to her ears in surprise at hearing the voice in her mind.

Me too. Wish I could have met my mother. Edwith, stepping forward politely, held out a paw and bowed his head so low that he overbalanced, fell on his snout, and bumped into Rachel.

Ooh, so sorry. I am so clumsy. I did not mean to scare you.

Shaking a little, Rachel smiled at him. "No, I was startled, that's all."

Nat turned to reassure his mother. "See? I told you he was a clown."

Although you can now hear us, you do not yet have the

ability to understand the Avalanyans. Jessynta pointed her wing at Pete. *Please explain the mind meld to your mother and introduce Mother Skyla who will accomplish it.*

Pete pointed to Skyla and her daughters. "This is Miss Skyla. She will mind-meld with you, and then you'll be able to understand and talk to them. You'll feel a little tingling, which doesn't hurt. It only has to be done once, and you'll be able to talk to any Avalanyan."

Skyla came forward and placed her hands on Rachel's temples.

Don't be afraid. I'm in contact with you mentally, but I'm not reading your mind, nor will I ever do so. This is merely a transferring of our language to you. It's different from the way the dragons communicate with us, as they have no spoken language.

Flinching a little at the tingling, Rachel relaxed when she heard Skyla's gentle voice.

"I admit when my boys told me what had been happening, I didn't believe any of it, but now here I am, and I don't think I'm dreaming. I'm Rachel, and I'm very pleased to meet you."

"I found it all slightly unbelievable too, although it was probably easier for me as I met the dragons at once, but it was all still a bit of a shock. Our children are quite an adventurous lot, aren't they? Meet Brecky, Izzy, and Lanya," said Skyla.

Rachel smiled at the girls. "Nice to meet you. I still feel like I'm dreaming. My boys love playing games, and I really expected your world to be more of the usual."

Edwith bounced up and down impatiently. *Enough of all this chattering. I am hungry. Let us begin the feast.*

Everyone laughed at his words.

The Avalanyans had come prepared for a beach picnic. Skyla spread mats out and invited Rachel to sit. Seeing all the food, Rachel was surprised at the fruits she didn't recognize, along with nuts, cheeses, meats, and fresh fish.

"How do you like their bread? Isn't it absolutely great? And such delicious butter. Wait until you taste their cream," said Nat. "Skyla has a farm."

"Skyla, did you make this cheese? It's so good, better than anything I've ever tasted. I wish I could get cheese like this back home." Rachel took another bite.

"We produce most of our food." Skyla handed her another chunk of cheese.

Edwith, who had been presented with an enormous haunch of venison, tore off a chunk of meat. Jessynta tapped his wing, and he dragged his meal off to eat a little distance from them.

Jessynta watched him go before beginning on her pile of fish, which she ate slowly.

Skyla nudged Rachel. "Did you see that? Jessynta must have felt that humans wouldn't feel comfortable with Edwith devouring raw meat while we're eating. She's even eating her fish more carefully than usual! She's so sweet."

For a while, everyone was quiet while they ate.

"I've never had a welcome like this before," Rachel said when she couldn't eat another bite.

Do you not honor mothers where you come from? Jessynta asked.

"We do, but I get the impression that it means more to you," said Rachel.

In our culture, mothers are the most important members of the family. They pass on their knowledge to their young before they are born. Then while in the egg, they transmit every piece of their heritage they can from deep memory back to the dawn of dragonkind. Dragonets come out of their shell with their genetic memory intact. And, of course, it knows its name, which I understand your kind does not. Because dragon mothers are the repositories of all knowledge, we revere them. Not that the father is not important, of course. In fact, he passes on his family history to the dragon in its egg as well. Between both parents, the dragonet learns as much history as it can.

Jessynta gazed out over the water. *In our case, it was rather a long time before we could be born because of the shape the world was in. This is why I am a little hazy about some of the things I ought to know. I remember more and more things as the days go by.*

"How did you do the lights in the cave? It looks great," Rachel said.

Deep at the bottom of our oceans, there is a lot of life with a natural fluorescence. I simply gathered as many as I could together, and the villagers made large glass bowls for me to put them in. Then I filled them with seawater and placed the creatures inside. The villagers can do much the same thing with little insects they call fireflies, and glowworms, but the glowworms do not like a lot of noise, so they are not so reliable. Jessynta preened herself with obvious delight at her cleverness.

Everyone praised her, which of course pleased her even more.

Edwith was anxious to have some of the praise. *Do not forget, Jessynta, I helped a lot as I am big and strong. I gathered the stones to make it more of a gentle slope so you would not have to climb over all those rocks at the entrance to the cave.*

Jessynta hung her head in embarrassment to have accepted all the praise. *Yes, you did do a great deal to help. I am sorry I did not credit you.*

Izzy and Nat gave Edwith a pat on his snout, making him purr like a very large cat.

"Why don't you come up to the farm, and we can chat some more?" Skyla started to clear the remains of the picnic.

Will jumped up, clapping his hands. "Do you hear that?"

Lanya immediately pointed up at the cliff behind her. "It's coming from up there behind our farm, but it's a little muffled."

I told you there was another dragon egg ready to hatch, said Edwith.

"There's an old volcano in the mountains behind where we

live. It's inactive, but as a healer, I often take sick people there to breathe in the fumes the crater gives off," said Skyla.

"It sounds interesting. Is it far?" Rachel asked.

"It's a bit too far to go on foot, but we have horses. Jessynta, why don't you begin to swim the way we discussed? Wait for us by the towpath. We might be quite a while, so take your time and have a rest while you wait."

Hey, do not forget me. I cannot climb very fast, and I am not going in the water.

"We haven't forgotten," Izzy said.

Jessynta swam off. The others helped Edwith climb the cliff path.

At the top, Skyla pointed out the farm. "Here are the stables."

Rachel was delighted to see all the horses.

Skyla had a nice, brown mare saddled up for her. "Here's Sandy. She's very sweet. The girls will find gentle, sturdy ponies for your boys. I teach riding, so we'll put the boys on them while you have a practice ride around the yard. Girls, give the boys a few tips. Show them what to do and how to sit straight. Don't worry; there won't be any jumping or galloping, so all you have to do is relax and enjoy."

Saddled up, they trotted slowly around until Skyla determined the boys were relaxed enough to begin the journey. "Okay! Now get down, and we can load up."

The girls gathered ropes and sturdy shoes in case they had to climb slippery slopes.

"We've also packed a lot of water and food, because I've no idea how long it will take to find the egg," said Skyla.

The cart stood ready, waiting for horses to be hitched to it. They were a little spooked by Edwith. One reared up and galloped away, trembling as soon as he saw the dragon.

I am not going to eat you, Edwith said defensively.

"Why don't you lie down and make yourself as small as you can, and I'll bring another? Here is our quietest one." Skyla brought a horse to Edwith, stroking its muzzle and talking to it very gently. The horse bent its head and snuffled Edwith.

Ooh that tickles. Edwith squished himself as small as he could.

Skyla patted the horse very gently and whispered quietly in its ear while leading it to the cart. She quickly hitched him and another horse to it. A few more treats and gentle words from Skyla soon settled them down.

It does not look very comfortable. Could you put some straw in the bottom for me? You did say it was a long way.

The girls gathered bundles of straw and spread it on the cart floor.

"Edwith, you're always telling us how strong you are. I don't think the journey would be too long for you," said Brecky.

My paw pads are still on the tender side. I could walk at first then climb in if I get sore paws. Let me test the cart anyway.

Without warning, he took a flying leap but misjudged the distance. The cart toppled over, spilling the carefully packed supplies and spooking the horses yet again.

"Oh, really, Edwith! Now we have to start over again," exclaimed Skyla.

Rubbing his snout, he looked rather embarrassed.

Izzy broke into giggles and the others joined in. Edwith laughed too; he never seemed to mind being laughed at.

Wait until I finally get airborne. I will be so strong and graceful, you will see. I am not designed to walk on the ground.

With everyone helping, they soon had everything repacked. The girls took Rachel and the children to the stable and the ponies they had tried out earlier.

Nat climbed into the saddle eagerly. He kicked gently at his pony's sides, trying to gallop to the front as he gained confidence. "Bet you can't catch me!"

Will promptly chased after him. "That's what you think!"

Pete, who regarded himself as the most sensible of the

three, caught up with them. "What are you doing? We're not here for play. We're going on a search. Look! Mum's waving to us, and she doesn't look too happy."

Rachel, who had already mounted Sandy, shouted at them. "Pete's right. Look at the other ponies. One of them has his ears laid back; that means he's frightened."

One of the others neighed in alarm as the boys rode the ponies closer to the dragons.

"I'm pleased you're comfortable riding but slow down," said Skyla. "Talk quietly to them, and let the girls give them apple pieces as you bring them closer to the cart."

Nat's pony became very skittish, and he nearly fell off.

Rachel scolded Nat and Will. "You see what happens if you play around too much. You could get hurt if you fall."

"Sorry, Mum. I just got excited," said Nat.

"I'm sorry too," said Will as he quietly reined in his pony.

"Children, walk your ponies behind the cart," said Skyla.

Finally everything was ready. Edwith climbed into the cart carefully.

Pete patted his pony's head. "This is even better than I thought it would be. My pony is so gentle."

"Me too," agreed Nat. "I'd really like to have lessons. Wouldn't you, Will?"

"Maybe, but all I can think about right now is the dragon waiting for me. I hope we get there soon."

After two hours, they reached the base of the volcano and tied the animals to a hitching post.

Edwith climbed down from the wagon without upsetting anything but promptly showed off by clambering up the side of the mountain in short bunny hops. Jessynta arrived in time to see Edwith jumping up and down at the base of the volcano waving his wings. She walked over very quietly, careful not to come too close to the horses.

How do you like my new trick? he asked her. *I know I am not very good at it yet, but I have not been trying for long. Soon I will be able to take flight if there is somewhere to launch from. Then just you wait and see. I am sure I shall fly quite beautifully. When we reach the top, I will show you by flying all the way down this little hill.*

Do not dare, scolded Jessynta. *You are not to risk hurting yourself at his stage of your development. Your wing struts are not strong enough yet.*

I do not see why not. How do you know anyway? I have not seen you even try.

That is quite enough cheek from you, young Edwith! I have a good mind to ground you for a couple of moons. I have my mother's memories, and she shared the mechanics of flight for dragons with me.

Brecky was surprised. "I assumed you couldn't fly in the air at all because your wings are so small."

I am not yet mature enough to be able to levitate and swim through the airwaves. Like Edwith, I need practice and more time. However, if I move slowly, I can make my way up this hill.

"Your dragons are full of themselves, aren't they?" remarked Rachel very quietly to her sons. "But they really are rather spectacular creatures."

As they climbed higher, the air around them cooled, but they stayed warm from the exertion. They were glad for the water stops.

Will took off, scrambling up the volcano in a hurry. "We're coming. Yes, I know you're hurting, and it's a tight fit in there, but we're going to get to you very soon, I promise."

Then he looked at the others. "Now I know how you felt when you first heard your dragons. It's for real! I'm being called. His voice isn't like Jessynta and Edwith's. He sounds all warm and fuzzy somehow. He's pleading with me to hurry."

Lanya gave Will a fist bump. "His name is Rayvinith! I can hear him too. He sounds as though something is muffling him, and he's upset."

Where exactly is his egg? asked Jessynta. *Will and Lanya, please lead the way, but do be careful. We are approaching the top now, and the crust is very thin. Go slowly when you start down. In fact, I do not think it will hold Edwith and me. We will wait for you here.*

Pete frowned. "This looks really dangerous, and it smells awful, rather like rotten eggs."

"This is exactly like an old volcano I saw once in Italy near Mount Vesuvius. The ancient Romans used to take sick people there. It can be dangerous," said Rachel.

Skyla seemed completely unworried. "It'll be fine. I know this place well. Look. There's the roped off area. Don't go anywhere near the bubbling mud. Keep close to the edge."

"We can prod it with a stick like they do on snowy mountains," Nat suggested.

Rachel looked over the edge in alarm. "No, it could be dangerous leaning forward to poke at the crust. Where's the voice coming from, Will?"

"Over there on the far side. We don't need to cross at all. If we keep to the sides, we should be all right. I think he's calling from that cave a little way past that wall of crust."

"I can feel him a lot stronger now too, and he's so anxious. We're on our way, Rayvinith," Lanya called out.

Rayvinith

CHAPTER ELEVEN

EVERYONE BEGAN VERY CAUTIOUSLY to cross the sandy crust, hugging the edge behind Will and Lanya. The dragons followed, keeping to the rim above them. Reaching the other side, they came to a small cave in the wall of the rim. As they drew closer, a blast of heat hit them.

"Phew! I know people go into these caves for a health cure, but I wouldn't be able to stay in one very long myself," said Izzy.

Wincing and covering their ears, Will and Lanya stopped just inside the entrance.

"Please, not so loud, Rayvinith," said Will. "We're here. Come on, Lanya."

They approached the large, brightly glowing, red egg. Will and Lanya felt very carefully around the top and found a slight depression but could not get a grip anywhere to pull. The dragonet inside began to moan.

Will's eyes grew wide with panic. "He's so upset. What can we do to help him, Lanya?"

Lanya tapped on the shell. "Please, Rayvinith, don't cry. We're trying to free you. Can you push from inside?"

Rachel stepped forward, holding up her hammer. "Time to use this. I'll tap the shell carefully."

"Are you sure you won't hurt him?" Lanya asked.

"I learned how to do this when I was out looking for fossils and bones in my days as a geologist." She tapped very gently, and a crack appeared around the indentation. The shell began opening, and everybody came close to help pull the shell apart. Small pieces fell off, and a shiny, glistening membrane came into view.

"Oh, that looks like the covering around a newborn animal, but it must be thicker than normal," said Skyla. "We must tear it off quickly to let him breathe."

As soon as they had cleared the pieces of shell away, they tore at the tough membrane.

Will exclaimed, "No wonder his voice sounded so fuzzy. He was so tightly wrapped up in this skin-like thing!"

Finally, they released the dragonet from its covering, and an exhausted, fiery red dragonet was revealed, standing on rather wobbly legs. He promptly burst into huge, crocodile tears.

At last! I am so glad to see you, William and Guillanya. My name is Rayvinith, and I have been trapped in this egg for ages, and awful things have happened since my mother laid me. By this time, he was sobbing almost uncontrollably.

Will and Lanya hurriedly placed their hands on his head, feeling the burn the others had felt at the moment of bonding. Then, seeing how upset he was, they hugged him close, putting their arms around him as tightly as they could.

Pete was worried. "What's the matter with him, Jessynta? You and Edwith weren't like this."

Jessynta had very carefully come closer once the dragonet was out of his shell, but Edwith remained on the upper rim.

Welcome to Avalanya, Rayvinith. Now tell us what has been happening and why you are so upset.

I was asleep in the beginning. I dreamed of a beautiful world with animals playing, and birds singing and lots of friendly humans, some even riding on us. Everybody was happy. Those were the good dreams; then came the nightmares. Humans fighting with each other, chopping down whole forests, burning lots of nasty smelling stuff, and travelling in smelly, noisy machines. Then came the earth shakes, and I was rocking and rocking violently, sometimes tumbling over and over. I was burning hot and sometimes almost freezing, even inside my egg. I called out to see if there were any other eggs or even dragons around, but nothing answered, and I knew I was alone in the world with no more humans. There would not be anyone around to help me hatch. I kept losing consciousness, and after what seemed like thousands of years, I gave up. I do not remember anything more until I sensed you, William and Guillanya. Am I still dreaming? Please promise not to go away.

He trembled violently as he clung even harder to them.

You really have had a rough time in your egg, said Jessynta. It is most unusual, as you should have had your mother telling you her life memories and histories. Something must have happened to her. We probably will never know what. Calm down and let the humans help you down this mountainside.

Will yelled, "My stomach! Rayvinith must be doing it."

"Mine too." Lanya was doubled over in pain.

Please, I really am most awfully hungry. Could you find me something to eat?

Oh, you poor thing. We should have known better, especially Edwith. He is always eating.

Hey, not so much of that, my fine friend. I will see if I can find a small animal or creature for him, maybe a rabbit.

All of you, do not forget to gather the shell pieces while I catch fish for our new friend.

"There's food in the cart, but I'm sure he will be able to eat more if you don't mind," Brecky said.

Jessynta slithered down the sloping side of the volcano.

I will make sure there is food for you, Rayvinith. I know what it is like to be hungry. Edwith's voice was heard although he was out of sight.

The descent for everyone else was quite tiring. Rayvinith was unable to go very fast, so they took turns carrying him. Luckily, he was only the size of a very large dog.

By the time they reached the bottom of the volcano, they were all exhausted and glad Jessynta and Edwith were waiting with a pile of fish and a small rabbit. Skyla and Rachel emptied the cart of the food, while Rayvinith fell upon it, helped by Edwith, of course.

In the bright sun, the dragonet's fiery red scales and feather-tipped wings began to dry out. They glistened and were shot with oranges, yellows, and golds. He seemed to be on fire.

"He looks like South American pictures of their sacred dragons or maybe like the dinosaur Archaeopterix." Will watched Edwith gulp down another large fish. "Edwith, don't be greedy. If you eat too much, there won't be room in the cart for everybody."

Lanya asked Rayvinith, "Have you had enough to eat? You can sit in the cart. Edwith will look after you."

Are you and William not coming with me then? He sobbed loudly and great flames shot out of his mouth, narrowly missing Edwith. *Make it stop! Help me, help me!*

Watch it, shrieked Edwith in dismay. *I am certainly not going to travel with you. Even though I still find walking hard, it will be better than being roasted alive!*

Then Skyla took charge. "This absolutely will not do. You two must get control of yourselves at once. Edwith, we should have made you walk sooner. You can walk or hop or whatever you like, but this behavior must stop at once. The best thing will be for Lanya and Will to ride with Rayvinith and keep him calm. The ponies will follow the others behind the cart."

Skyla spoke to the queen dragon. "Jessynta, try to sort Rayvinith and his fears out, as we cannot risk him setting fire to everything," Skyla said.

Rayvinith, I know you are scared but try as best you can, and

I will help you soon. William and Guillanya can take care of you now but try to control your flame. Face outward over the edge of the cart. We shall have a long talk when we meet at the farm. Edwith, no fooling around on the way. You are an experienced dragon now, and I expect good behavior. I will swim and meet you back on the beach.

Yes, madam, I will try hard.

Do not be cheeky.

By the time they were finally ready to set off, Rayvinith had calmed down and settled quietly in between Will and Lanya in the cart. After a slightly slower journey, because Edwith had to work hard to keep up with them, they reached the farm.

Rayvinith was quite subdued while he waited for the humans to unload and return the horses and ponies to the stables. Everybody went down to the beach. Rayvinith very quietly allowed himself to be half-carried, and half-led to where Jessynta was waiting by a cave. Edwith, rather chastened by Jessynta's stern words earlier managed to make it to the beach reasonably calmly.

Rayvinith looked at Jessynta. *What is that cave? Is that where I will sleep?*

Lanya looked thoughtful. "That's a good point. Have we got time to choose another cave for him, Jessynta?"

Another cave? Will I have to sleep alone then? Please do not make me do that. Can I not sleep with William and Guillanya? Rayvinith sank onto the sand in front of Jessynta's cave, resting his head on his paws dejectedly.

You have to come and see my cave. It is a lot bigger than Jessynta's. There will be more room for the two of us. Edwith bounced around excitedly.

Izzy tugged her mother's arm. "You let us have Edwith in our stable when he arrived. Perhaps we could take care of Rayvinith there."

Skyla shook her head. "It would be better for him to sleep

with one of the dragons. Besides, he could set fire to the hay in the stables. Let's take him to Edwith's cave."

The group made their way there. Edwith hopped, skipped, and tumbled at the head of the parade.

Edwith touched Rayvinith's wing when they arrived. *Look at my pretty shells and moss I found yesterday.*

It is dark in here, remarked Rayvinith.

Edwith spun in a circle, taking in his cave. *Can you get me some lights, Jessynta? I will trade you some of my nice moss.* He tapped his chin with a claw. *It would of course be a lot prettier if I could find sparkly ornaments.*

"If you like sparkly things, I could look in our local shops tomorrow," said Rachel.

Delighted, Edwith jumped several feet off the ground, hit the roof of the cave, misjudged the landing, and fell on his tail. Everyone laughed, including Rayvinith, who unfortunately coughed out a flame, just missing Edwith.

Ouch! shrieked Edwith. *I am not so sure about sharing my lovely cave with you now, Rayvinith.*

Right, that settles it. This is my final word. Jessynta stamped her foot. *Edwith, we will settle Rayvinith in your cave. Rachel and the boys must soon be on their way.*

Tears threatened again in Rayvinith's eyes. *On their way. What do you mean? How long is it going to be before I see you again?* He clung to Will and Lanya.

This is all a little hard for you to understand, Rayvinith, but we will have a good talk when you are settled, said Jessynta.

Will let out a loud groan.

I am hungry, Rayvinith said.

I am ravenous too. It has been ages since we ate, said Edwith petulantly.

Lanya winced and rubbed her stomach.

I am sorry. I must lessen your bonds a little. We cannot have you hurting every time Rayvinith is hungry, said Jessynta.

Lanya's eyes opened wide in surprise. "You can do that?"

Yes, I will work on it tomorrow. Try deep breathing and relax. In the meantime, we will get Rayvinith settled. Edwith, find him a snack or two to tide him over. I am sure you have some tidbits stashed away.

How do you know that?

Jessynta gave him a withering look.

I will fetch something for him. He disappeared into the dark recesses at the back of his cave, returning quickly with meat scraps for Rayvinith.

Rayvinith swallowed them whole, then gave a large burp accompanied by a huge gout of flame, causing everyone to scatter out of his way. *Ooh help me! What is happening? I am on fire again. Please, make it stop.*

He tried to hide behind Will, who was trying to console him while avoiding the flames.

Now come, young Rayvinith. Stop that at once. You will hurt the humans. We are different types of dragons. Edwith is an air dragon, and I am a water dragon. You are a fire dragon, so naturally, you breathe flames and smoke. However, these skills have to be learnt gradually, and you will have to work at it. You will not burn yourself, but you have to be careful. You could injure others around you. You must concentrate on relaxing. Now come, Rayvinith, breathe very slowly at first. Do not panic.

But I do not like it. Where is it coming from?

You will learn by experimenting. Fire dragons have an extra stomach in which the fire is generated, and you have to learn how to use and control it.

Rayvinith shrieked, *Oh, no! I am sure I will not want to do that.*

You will have to. I am certain you will learn in time, but for now, just be very careful, especially after eating, as that seems to trigger it. In the meantime, let us go outside into the light.

Outside the cave, Rachel's eyes drooped as she tried to

stifle a yawn. "I'm so tired. What's the time?" She glanced at her watch. "Something's gone wrong with it."

"Our digital things don't work here, possibly because there are no satellites. Time passes differently too," Pete explained.

"You boys are going to have a hard time without the use of your screens then! So how do they tell the time here?" she asked.

"We haven't really had much time to sort out things like that," said Pete. "I suspect they use sundials or water clocks."

Nat had an idea. "An old windup watch might work. They don't use a battery."

Pete didn't look impressed. "I don't think that's a good idea. Things could get very complicated. None of it would synchronize with our world anyway, so it really doesn't matter. I vote that we just go along with whatever Jessynta says."

Rachel suddenly collapsed onto the sand. "I can't take any of that in at the moment. I'm exhausted and too tired to even think."

Pete looked closely at her, noting dark circles under her eyes. "We really must leave as soon as we can."

Rayvinith shrieked, batting his feathered wings at Will. *No please do not go I still do not know where I will be sleeping.*

Will gently patted Rayvinith's head. "Look, Lanya is here, and she can help you to settle in." He pointed to the moss. "See all that? How about we help you make a bed with it?"

I will help. Edwith bossed them around until he had arranged the décor to his satisfaction.

Jessynta had been quiet for a while but finally said, *I have been checking my memories again, and I think our time anomaly is affecting your mother. She has spent a little too long here for her first day. You should take her home.*

Pete's face fell. "Does that mean she can't come here again?"

Not at all. Just that she and your father should be careful how much time they spend here. They need to be well rested.

Adults are affected much more by the time anomaly than you children.

Rachel was yawning when Skyla helped her to her feet. "Goodbye for now. You must get home and get a good sleep. I hope to see you again before too long."

Rayvinith began to cry again, especially when the sobs made him produce a little flame.

Will's heart went out to him. "Rayvinith, please don't cry. I must go. Jessynta will explain why we can't stay. There are a few problems with time between our worlds, but you'll get used to it."

After a last extra big hug, Will left while Rayvinith turned around and around on his moss like a large puppy.

The boys helped their sleepy mother back to the original cave. By the time they got back home, she was almost asleep on her feet, so the boys busied themselves getting a cup of tea for her.

Dropping down onto the nearest chair, their mother remarked, "It's probably good Dad isn't at home at the moment. I just don't have enough energy to explain today's events to him. I feel like it's all been a dream."

"Well don't worry about it. We feel the same, and we've been several times now," said Nat. "In fact, if it wasn't for the slight buzzing in my mind, which must be my connection to Edwith, I might think I had dreamed it as well."

"I feel something from Rayvinith too," Will said.

When everyone had finished eating, Pete suggested they take it easy for the afternoon. "Mum, why don't you take a nap while we clear up? I admit I feel a little saddle sore myself."

"If nobody minds, I will do that. Have a quiet afternoon yourselves."

CHAPTER TWELVE

AS SOON AS THEY had cleared the table, Pete went up to see if their mother needed anything. She was sound asleep, so he closed her door quietly, collected some shell pieces, and joined his brothers in the main room.

"Now would be a good time to get out our shells. Mum is sound asleep. Sit here on the sofa."

Will anxiously searched his pockets. "Oh! I left the sack with pieces of Rayvinith's shell behind in Edwith's cave. I won't be able to reach him."

Pete reassured him with a smile. "Don't worry. He's probably still too confused." He and Nat gave Will a piece of their shells, and they held them close. After only a few seconds, they all heard Jessynta's voice.

Hallo. How is your mother?

"She was very tired but feels better now that she's home. She's taking a nap," said Pete.

"Will forgot his shells. He wanted to try talking with Rayvinith," Nat said.

He is too new to everything, so I have not told him about shell communication. It took a while to get him settled. It is actually a good thing William cannot talk directly to him. He is having trouble with his flaming, but Edwith is trying to help, although he does tend to make him laugh, which starts up the flames again. We will have to come up with ideas next time we meet to get him used to the fire. I never heard of a fire dragon who was frightened of his own flame. However, I suppose he did miss out learning such a lot from his mother. I left Edwith and the girls with him. Lanya sings to him. In fact, Edwith singing along with her was making Rayvinith laugh!

Nat laughed. "I should love to have heard him! Wouldn't you, Will?"

"You bet. Without the flames, of course." Will smiled.

William, I heard you earlier talking about dinosaurs and one in particular in your world. I think you called it an Archaeopterix. Rayvinith could be related to it. According to my genetic memories, there was one like that here. We dragons are all descended from a distant branch of dinosaurs.

Will gasped. "You had dinosaurs too? Did an asteroid hit your world?"

No, an asteroid did not hit our world. Dinosaurs did not evolve directly into dragons. We were a separate branch of their family tree. Our dinosaurs died out gradually because our world got a lot cooler, and the vegetation they relied on died out. They grew too big for the amount of food sources available. As we became larger ourselves, we took over as the largest land animals. Pete nudged Nat. "Now that would interest our scientists. How do dragons know about our ancient past?"

As a queen, my mother is descended from a very long line of genetic memories, and many centuries ago, dragons visited your world. The telling of that story will take longer than we have time for now.

Pete and Nat looked at each other.

Will gave them a satisfied grin. "See! I knew dragons could be related to dinosaurs. Maybe ancient humans saw them when they visited our world."

"You really can surprise us," said Pete. "Our scientists have puzzled over the dinosaurs for ages, but somehow, I don't think they would believe us if we told them what you told us."

I do have to go now and help the others but hope it will not be too long before your next visit. Her voice faded away.

"If humans saw dragons, that could explain why we have so many tales about monsters," said Nat.

"A dragon like Jessynta could have easily started the Loch Ness monster tales," admitted Pete.

Will rested his chin on his hands. "That's all very well, but we have something more important to think about now. Poor Rayvinith and his fear of fire." Then his eyes lit up. "I know. What about some sort of game? A competition to see who could shoot flames the farthest?"

"Do you suppose that Edwith can shoot flames? We know Jessynta can, because she flamed the fish," said Pete.

Nat laughed out loud. "Imagine us trying to teach dragons how to breathe fire. That's a hoot, isn't it?"

"Sure is." Will gave Nat a high five.

Pete looked at his watch. "It's not too late to go down to the shops now. I saw lots of decorated shells. Some even had sequins stuck on them."

Nat added, "I saw long chains with sparkly glass stones."

Pete laughed. "We'll have to look for jewelry. I also saw fake badges with shiny stones on them. It really won't matter how gaudy they are--the more glitter the better. The dragons will like them. Charms, gold painted shells, anything glittery will do. They even liked the gold and silver foil wrapped around the candy."

Will clapped excitedly. "Ornaments of any kind to put on necklaces to give the winner a prize. It should encourage competition. Quick. Let's go before the shops close."

They ran down to the souvenir shops and were delighted to find a lot of very cheap, gaudy necklaces, brooches, and even a few brass chains. They returned home highly delighted.

Their mother was making a cup of tea, and they shared

their idea with her. "You've been busy, but I do see the point of it. I had planned to look for more of the same. It's a pity we aren't at home, as I could find stuff more easily, but I'll see what I can find."

She took her cup to the table and sat down, sighing happily. "I really love your dragons. Jessynta seems very wise for a newborn creature. I feel it's possible to put my full trust in her, which is somewhat surprising considering, only the other day, I had no belief in dragons whatsoever. I don't know why I feel this way. Perhaps the out-of-world experience has changed me. Skyla seems very sensible, so I'm sure that, between them, they will ensure you come to no harm when you're there."

Pete raised his eyebrows at her remark. "That's a relief. I thought you'd be worried when we go on our own. So you won't mind us setting off early tomorrow?"

"No, not at all. I will do a little shopping while you're gone."

~~~~~

The next day, after gobbling down breakfast, the boys ran eagerly to the top of the hill, hauling their bags of goodies with them. Leaving the cave, they were met by three very excited dragons.

Will was nearly knocked over. "Hi, Rayvinith, did you have a good night in Edwith's cave?"

We are so excited to see you. It always seems like such a long time, said Jessynta.

Edwith turned a somersault, getting really close to Will and Rayvinith, causing them to jump.

Hey, be careful! I might accidentally flame you if you startle me too much! said Rayvinith.

Nat ignored Edwith's antics and addressed Jessynta. "It works out well for us, because after a night's sleep, we get up and come here. Only one night as gone by on our world, although we do get a little rundown."
~~~~~

Eventually they all calmed down and were able to greet the girls who had watched the proceedings with grins.

Izzy pouted. "We never get that kind of greeting."

You do not leave for such a long time, and we are never sure when the boys will come again, said Jessynta.

Rayvinith leaned against Will. *Jessynta and Edwith explained a lot more to me, and they have really been looking after me. Guillanya has been lovely. She gave me a bath in the sea and rubbed sweet-smelling oil on my skin.*

About time too, said Edwith. *He smells of smoke and makes the cave stink. I might even have to take a dip myself.* He shuddered. *We are going to have to work on this fire thing.*

"We have some ideas to discuss with you," said Nat. "We've thought about how to help him, and Will has come up with at least one idea for a fun game. Can you breathe fire, Edwith?"

I suppose so, although I have not ever tried.

It is an instinct shared by all dragons. We have an extra stomach, although fire dragons have a bigger one. Why? asked Jessynta.

"You mentioned once while flaming fish for us to eat that you thought you'd eaten enough to produce a small flame. Is there anything special that can be eaten to start the fire going?"

Yes, there are rocks which are high in phosphorus, and if we eat them, it should help. I do not think that Rayvinith would need to eat much, because he can naturally produce fire.

Will looked at Jessynta. "Can you find a few of those rocks for us to experiment with?"

She nodded and set off with Edwith along the edge of the cliff to search. It wasn't long before there was a small pile of rocks in front of each dragon.

"Now try eating some of them, including you, Rayvinith," said Pete.

Oh, must I? I really do not like even the little flames I produce by accident, let alone making more, he whimpered.

We will help you. It is the first time for Edwith too. Do not be frightened. This is natural for you, I promise. Come along now. You can do it. Jessynta pushed rocks closer to the still whimpering dragon and chomped a few herself.

But Rayvinith's head still drooped. Lanya patted him on the back. "Why don't you go to the edge of the sea before you swallow a piece of the rock. The water might help if you overdo it."

He finally picked up a tiny piece of the rock in his front claw and, encouraged by Will and Lanya, put it in his mouth. He let out a loud shriek.

Ouch, that hurt!

"What hurt?" asked Will.

I bit my tongue.

"Oh, dear. Just try again and be more careful."

It is all very well for you. You are not trying to chew hard rocks.

Jessynta was the first dragon to produce a flame.

Brecky opened her eyes wide. "My goodness, that is a lot bigger than your flame for cooking. You'd better aim it out to sea."

Pete jumped back from the dragon. "That flame must be about two meters in length. This could be dangerous for us. We'd better keep well back."

Edwith gobbled his rocks as fast as he could. *I can do better than that measly flame.*

"Now, Rayvinith," chorused the children. "Ready, go!"

The poor little dragon fell over backward in fright at the gout of flame which shot out of his mouth. He swallowed a large amount of seawater, causing him to choke and splutter.

Please, that is enough. I do not like it. I really do not.

Come on now, Rayvinith. You did not hurt yourself, and your flame was not anywhere as long as mine. You are supposed to be a fire dragon, and you cannot even squirt a decent flame, said Edwith.

That is quite enough teasing from you, said Jessynta.

Izzy called from a safe distance, "Yes, I agree, Jessynta. We all must help him. Unfortunately, it must be by trial and error. Have another go.

I did not expect to be able to project my flame far, because I have so much water in my body. No matter how much of that rock I eat, I would never be able to manage more than a small amount. I am pleased with what I achieved though. So, William, what do you suggest now? What is your idea? asked Jessynta.

"For the moment, we can continue just doing this until Rayvinith can spout a flame at least as far as Jessynta."

Ignoring Rayvinith's protests, Will urged him to eat one mouthful at a time. "Come on, you can do it. Munch, crunch, munch and crunch."

After a while, Rayvinith managed to emit a small flame without falling over.

That is enough. I did one. Let me drink water. My stomach feels hot.

I do not think that is a very good idea, as it will spoil your attempts to produce fire. That is, after all, the whole point of this exercise, scolded Jessynta.

Rayvinith turned his back to her. *I told you I do not like it.*

Come now, young Rayvinith, make me proud of you. Try and make a flame to match those gorgeous red wing feathers.

"Please, Rayvinith, try some more. We've planned a surprise for you if you do well." said Will.

Very reluctantly, he timidly opened his mouth and breathed out a very tiny flame with only a slight flinch.

"That is fantastic!" praised Lanya.

Will patted him gently on the back, being very careful to stay behind the dragon.

"Now do it again a teeny bit harder," Pete encouraged.

Edwith said, *Way to go, young Rayvinith. Keep it up and you might soon be able to compete with me.*

Rayvinith tried again, getting the flame a little farther each time but was still very cautious.

Is that enough? Can I stop now?

"Oh no, we are just getting started. Besides, we haven't even begun the game yet," replied Will.

The three dragons continued swallowing rocks and breathing fire for several more minutes.

"We are going to make this a competition. I'm going to put a stick out in front of you, and when I say go, you must try your hardest to breathe out fire," said Will. "There is a surprise for the winner."

What is it? asked Edwith.

"I'm not telling, as it wouldn't be a surprise then, would it?" Will walked five yards away and put a stick in the sand. He drew a line for each dragon to stand on. "Right, now for a trial. We'll allow Edwith to be first."

Edwith swallowed several chunks of the rock and puffed out his chest. Then, taking a big breath, he spat out a long stream of fire. Although it was in fact close to the stick, he was quite upset not to have reached the target.

That was just a practice. I will try again.

"No, you won't. One turn at a time is how it will go," said Will.

Jessynta was next, and although hers was better than her previous efforts, she was way behind Edwith.

"Now it's your turn, Rayvinith," said Will. "Don't let Lanya and me down. Eat a few more rocks, and we'll stand well back and tell you when to go."

He took Lanya aside and whispered in her ear. "This isn't really fair, but we must shock him into it. So when I say 'ready steady,' shout *go* as loud as you can."

Rayvinith, looking very apprehensive, shuffled up to the starting line and, glancing back for reassurance, chomped down a mouthful of the rock and commenced chewing. He seemed to be finding it easier to grind the rock, judging by the noises he made eating. As soon as his pile of rocks was gone, he looked around pleadingly.

"Ready . . . steady," Will said.

"GO-o-o-ooooooooo!" yelled Lanya and Will in unison at the top of their voices. Poor Rayvinith nearly jumped out of his skin. When he opened his mouth in fright, out came the most gigantic flame they had seen that day, consuming the marker stick completely and singeing the seaweed for several meters past it.

He wasn't the only one who was frightened, as even Edwith fell on his tail after jumping several feet into the air.

Everyone burst into loud applause, even Edwith after he had righted himself. They rushed to hug Rayvinith and heap praises on him, not giving him a minute to cry out in fear. He had scarcely begun to squeal when Will produced a beautiful golden chain with a sparkling glass jewel from his backpack and offered it to Rayvinith.

"I pronounce you champion of the day," announced Will. "Take a bow."

Rayvinith was dumbstruck for several minutes.

Edwith cried, *I demand a rematch! That was unfair. You made him jump and that gave him a boost. Besides, I want a chance to win a prize too.*

Jessynta, too, had jumped a little in surprise. *I must say that was quite a shock you gave us, William and Guillanya. Rayvinith, that was very good but could you do it again? I do believe you could get it even farther.*

Rayvinith was quiet for a few minutes as he pawed his lovely prize. *You really gave me such a shock, my nerves are almost shot to pieces. But I cannot help feeling a little proud of myself for scoring such a victory. But please, do not do that again. I could have died of fright!*

I still think it was not fair, and I would like a chance to win a prize. Have you got any more?

"Yes, we have," answered Will. "What about it, Rayvinith?

Now you know you can do it, and you didn't burn yourself. Would you like to try again? This time we promise not to make you jump. You just spout the flame when you're ready."

It was agreed that all three dragons would have another go, even Jessynta, because she needed the practice too.

"Why don't you all line up and go together. That will give you a chance to see how your powers match," said Brecky.

The dragons lined up with a good-sized space between them, and Pete placed a new stick several paces farther than the last time.

Jessynta had to find a few more rocks first. Pete and Brecky went with her to carry them in a sack. While she was gone, Edwith decided to warm up. He was so serious that the others laughed at his antics. He kept taking huge breaths and puffing himself up.

As soon as the fresh supply of rocks was delivered to their feet, Pete suggested a total of three tries each to make it fair. The dragons ate as much as they thought necessary, although Rayvinith hardly ate any rock at all.

Pete began the count. "On my count. ONE, TWO, THREE!"

The dragons blasted forth massive flames. Edwith succeeded in beating Rayvinith but only just.

See! I told you I could beat you. Edwith bowed to the claps from the children.

For the next round, he chomped in earnest, devouring his entire pile in three gulps. However, just as Pete gave the countdown, he regurgitated a messy pile of gray mud, leaving the field to Rayvinith and Jessynta. This time, Rayvinith won, but surprisingly, Jessynta made her best effort yet.

Edwith groaned in pain and rolled on the ground, gasping and retching. He couldn't seem to stop, and he regurgitated more and more mud, panting with pain. Brecky and Izzy ran to get their mother to see if she knew of anything to calm his stomach.

Jessynta seemed to be okay, although she said her throat was a little sore. Rayvinith didn't have any problems and was strutting around in delight when he suddenly developed hiccups. Each time he hiccupped, a small flame came out of his mouth, once almost setting fire to Lanya's tunic. She and Will moved rapidly out of his reach. Rayvinith didn't seem to be at all frightened of his flame now but complained about the hiccups.

Lanya pointed to a small waterfall coming out of the nearby cliff and told him to drink some water until they stopped.

While all this was going on, Jessynta sat very quietly, deep in thought.

I think this is my fault, because I did not remember everything I should have from what my mother passed on to me. I knew about the rocks, but we are only supposed to munch a few now and then, or if we need to make a larger amount of fire than normal. So long as we eat a varied diet with foods rich in that phosphorus stuff, and we have a full stomach, we can breathe fire easily enough for most purposes. I do not think that Rayvinith really needs to eat many rocks at all, as he is a fire dragon. So long as he has a full stomach, he can spout plenty of flame. I was so excited about the game, I forgot. I am so sorry I spoke out before I had really thought it all through. She hung her head apologetically.

"I can understand you making mistakes now and then. It has been a very traumatic time for you all." Pete patted her gently. "But how can we help Edwith?"

"A lot of the blame must be mine, because I was the one who thought up the game," said Will.

Skyla arrived with the girls and a bag of herbs, soft bread, and a covered bucket of milk.

"It seems to me that Edwith completely overdid it and, in his eagerness to win a prize, ate far too much. I have some herbs here, to soothe upset stomachs." She crumbled the bread and mixed it into the milk with gingerroot. "Edwith, take small sips of this."

Oh no, my stomach hurts so much, I do not think I could swallow a thing. He collapsed onto the sand, weeping enormous crocodile tears.

Skyla patiently sat down beside him and, soaking a sponge in the concoction, dribbled a little at a time into his mouth while Izzy and Nat rubbed as much of his stomach as they could reach. Gradually he began to perk up enough to swallow some on his own, while everyone looked on anxiously. His scales were considerably paler than usual, almost yellow in fact.

Jessynta was still very quiet and forlorn about her mistake, but Rayvinith, although he sympathized with Edwith, was still pawing his prize.

After a while, Edwith was able to sit up and his scales began to get their color back.

Skyla said, "Edwith, you will really have to watch what you eat for the next few days. We will put you on a very soft diet. I'll go home and make up a nice meat broth for you, and I want you to eat a little of it every three or four hours until I'm sure your stomach has healed."

By this time, he had finished all the milk and bread and complained of the nasty taste in his mouth and his sore throat.

"I have one more thing I can give you to ease your throat." Producing jars of golden honey, she opened one of them. "I want you to take some of this now. Jessynta, you should as well. I have several jars so you can all have some.

Edwith was delighted with the taste, as were the others.

In a short while, the dragons were quite cheered up, although Edwith's stomach was still hurting him a bit.

"Now then, Edwith," said Will, "I don't want to rub this in, but you do realize that if you hadn't been so eager to beat everyone, you wouldn't have stuffed yourself so full of the rocks, right?"

"Yes," agreed Skyla. "You have a tendency to overdo things, don't you? So let this be a lesson to you. You are so big, but you're really still young and immature and have a lot to learn. Try to control yourself more."

Edwith hung his head.

Jessynta was very contrite and slumped back on her haunches. Skyla tried to comfort her. "You shouldn't blame yourself for everything that happens. Your mother had a great deal of knowledge. It's so much for you to remember."

"Why don't you kids come back to the farm and get something to eat while the dragons take a nap?" Skyla looked at the dragons. "Don't eat anything more for a while. I'll send something back with them later."

Before they left the beach, Pete emptied his backpack of the things he had found in the shop the night before and produced several more treasures.

"You may take turns to choose one," he told the dragons.

Rayvinith already had his. Edwith held back to let Jessynta choose first, which earned him a little pat on the nose from Nat.

After settling the dragons down in the soft sand for a short nap, Skyla and the children climbed the path and returned to the farmhouse. They went into the kitchen and helped Skyla put meat and broth into a very large pot to boil for Edwith to eat a bit later. "I meant what I said to Edwith. You must try to curb his exuberance, or one day, he could really get into trouble."

Izzy agreed. "I think he learned a valuable lesson today."

CHAPTER THIRTEEN

AT THE FARM, THE children sat down to eat snacks and drinks.

"Brecky, can you show us where your father found those old pieces he keeps in the shed? Is it far away?" asked Pete.

"It's just behind one of the barns. He was digging foundations for a new wall when the ground collapsed, and he found himself in a large hole."

"Let's go check it out." Will pushed away from the table.

When they reached the spot, large planks of wood covered the ground.

"Father wanted to protect what he had found from the weather, especially as most of it had already rotted away and fell to pieces when he touched it."

Together, the six children lifted the wood and looked down into a large hole. It looked like a room littered with a great many broken wooden boards. They carefully climbed down over the edge to search around. Part of an inner wall was covered with a large picture.

"We need more light." Pete took a torch out of his pocket and turned it on.

The girls were startled at the unexpected brightness. Brecky exclaimed, "What is that? Where did you get it? It gives off more light than the globes Jessynta gave us."

"It's a torch. I brought it from our world."

Izzy looked puzzled. "But how does it work? I don't see any sea creatures in it."

"It has a battery inside to give it power. The batteries don't last forever, so we have to replace them once in a while," said Nat.

"Point it at that picture on that broken wall over there." Izzy pointed to a large painting. "What's it covered in? I wonder why it hasn't gone rotten like everything else we have uncovered?"

"That stuff covering it looks like plastic," said Nat.

Izzy shrugged her shoulders. "What's plastic?"

"It's a material we use a great deal of in our world. It can preserve things," explained Pete.

Will went closer to look at it. "Look, Nat. This isn't a picture at all. It's just like those maps we see in our fantasy books. Could it be a map of this whole area before everything was destroyed?"

Nat traced his finger over areas of the picture. "There's a large land mass here. I don't understand any of the measurements, but those curving lines could show mountain height."

Will pointed to a wavy line. "There's a river marked there. Where that river is may be your coastline now. The sea could have flooded and cut the land in half, making it into an island."

Brecky turned up her nose. "The sea can't do that!"

He nodded his head. "Oh yes it could. Jessynta told us that the climate here changed centuries ago, and the sea flooded a lot of the land. That's what is happening in our world right now. The climate is changing. It's getting warmer, and the ice in our north is melting. That makes the sea rise. They say that a lot of low-lying land will get flooded. I read about it."

Pete smiled at him. "Yes, I know. You've always got your head in a book, but I've heard grownups talking about it as well. They're getting worried about it."

Will pointed. "Well that is where the sea is now. We went across it to the mountains to find Edwith."

Pete nodded. "And over the centuries, whatever your world was called before was forgotten, and people started calling the whole island Avalanya after the river which used to be there."

Brecky touched her sister's arm excitedly. "There are probably many ruined cities around our whole world. If only we had bigger boats, we could explore for other islands. Who knows? There could even be more dragon eggs, and they could be ready to hatch and bond."

Izzy hugged herself in delight. "When our dragons are strong enough to fly, perhaps we could ride on them. We could go and search."

Will shuddered. "Fly on dragons? No way. I don't think I could do that."

Nat grinned broadly, and his eyes shone. "I could. Like in our dragon books. What about you, Pete?"

But Pete had lost interest and was busy trying to unearth more things from the other side of the collapsed wall. He stared intently at a large object. "Look at this flat box. It could be some sort of computer." He brushed the dirt away to reveal a glass face. "It could be a screen. There are several wires tangled up on the floor."

Nat was still excited about the idea of flying and scoffed at him. "Mum always said you had a vivid imagination. You're getting carried away. They don't even have electricity. How could it be a computer?"

Pete frowned and looked angrily at his brother. "It's no crazier than your ideas of us flying off on our dragons to search."

Nat glared at his brother and shoved him. "Well, they have wings, and in our books, dragons fly. And with riders. So why shouldn't we?"

Pete shoved him back. "Use some sense. You're—"

Will grabbed his brothers. "Come on now. Please don't get into an argument. Let's get this map off the wall and take it up to the surface where there's better light, so we can have a good look at it."

Pete looked at Will's earnest face and calmed down. "You're right."

He helped Will and Nat ease the plastic away from the wall. They rolled the map up to carry it to the surface.

Climbing out of the hole and into the light, Pete looked more closely at the map. "Those mountains must have been much higher than they are now," said Pete.

"And there may be more things buried under our land if we dig around," said Izzy.

"That's just what our Earth archaeologists do," explained Nat. "But you have to do it very carefully, so as not to break things up, and you have to make a note of exactly where you found it."

Izzy frowned as she tripped up over the words "Arkywhatsits? What do they do?"

"They dig up old things and try to work out what happened in the past," Pete said.

Brecky grinned at her sister. "That's what we are doing."

Nat nodded. "That's what your father was doing too."

"We must really have a go at finding him." Izzy gazed at the map again. "Look there." She put a finger on another wavy line. "There's a river coming from the mountains. There's a word on it. I think it begins with an S and possibly an A at the end of the word. Perhaps that is the Staria River?"

Brecky touched her sister's arm. "Maybe those little black squiggles show houses where people once lived. They could be drawings of old villages or even those cities Jessynta talked about."

"Father heard of cities in the north, and there are more little squiggles further up. This picture shows more land up there, and that's the direction he took. I wonder if he found a city and people. But what would keep mother from being able to scry him for so long?"

"Let's tell Jessynta about this and see what she has to say. She may have memories she can search," said Pete.

They re-covered the hole to prevent more damage to the things inside it. Returning to the house, they showed Skyla what they had found.

"I knew your father had found many strange things and went to find an old city he had heard about from somebody. Nobody else believed it existed. Your uncle Aleto was fascinated by all kinds of old things he dug up. In fact, he wanted to go with your father, but Suki wouldn't let him. She had more sense than I did."

"I forgot about Ven and his parents. Let's go and visit him," said Will.

But Brecky shook her head. "I think it's a bit late to go there now. We can see him tomorrow."

"This picture thing is certainly intriguing. I'll have a good look at it while you check on the dragons," said Skyla.

She went to the fireplace and picked up a large covered bucket. "Take this soup with you. Make sure Edwith eats it very slowly, and here are some small scraps of meat for Rayvinith." Skyla filled Will's arms with a wrapped package.

As the children drew near the caves, they saw the dragons sunning themselves on the beach. Edwith woke up when they approached with the soup.

I smell food, he announced in delight as the other two dragons lazily stretched themselves. *I feel better already. My stomach is rumbling with hunger.*

"You're recovering very fast, Edwith," said Izzy. "But mother says you must eat it slowly."

I will, I promise. I really do not want to go through anything like that again.

As they put the bucket down in front of him, Jessynta swam out to sea to catch fish.

"Mother sent more jars of honey and herbs for you all in case your throats are still a little sore," said Brecky.

Edwith licked his large mouth with a huge green tongue.

"Edwith, as your inside was the most harmed, I'll bring another bucket of soup for you in a couple of hours. You're absolutely not to eat any solid food for at least the rest of today. The meat is for you, Rayvinith."

Rayvinith coyly bowed his head in thanks.

A much-chastened Edwith meekly agreed to do as he was told. When Jessynta returned with her fish, they sat down to tell the dragons about their latest discovery.

Jessynta was very interested to hear about the map and the ruins. She agreed there must have been a lot more land around when she was in the egg.

I think we may be able to search for your father when we are a little more mature and have learned to fly properly. It will take a great deal of preparation, and we have a lot more to learn about our skills. We shall have to start practicing as soon as Edwith has recovered. Both he and Rayvinith must strengthen their wings every day. I have to admit that Edwith is growing really fast, and now that Rayvinith is no longer quite so scared of fire, he should be able to reach his full potential in a few weeks' time. I too have a deal of remembering to do before I am able to fly.

"You will be careful though, won't you?" said Lanya "After all, Rayvinith only just began to breathe fire, and even though you are all so big and growing so fast, you are very young dragons. No more fire breathing for a few more days."

Will was very relieved to see how much better Rayvinith was. "I don't really think that applies to you. Now that you can flame without so much fear, you can experiment and see how long you could flame without eating those rocks. What do you think, Jessynta?"

We can help him by setting him little tasks and games like you did, William, and I will not let Edwith open his mouth.

Edwith meekly nodded his agreement.

Lanya looked at him, then patted Rayvinith. "It will be good for you to keep on practicing until you have complete control."

He put his head down on the sand, and she gave him a little hug. "Don't look miserable. You're doing well."

Will went over to give him a hug as well. "Try not to worry about it. By the time I see you again, who knows how far you'll be able to shoot your flames. I'll look for more prizes."

Rayvinith's eyes lit up when he heard that.

To Pete, Will added, "I'm also relieved I won't have to try flying for a while."

"Don't worry so much about flying. I'm sure you'll be fine." Pete looked at the sky. "I think we should be going. We have been here ages." He turned toward Edwith who still had his snout buried in the bucket. "I hope you recover and are back to normal soon."

Edwith looked up quickly, whipping his head around with an open mouth full of soup, nearly drenching Pete. Pete jumped backward. "Hey, don't drool your soup all over me."

Nat was just about to give Edwith a hug but, seeing his face covered in soup, stepped back quickly. "I love you, Edwith, but I think I'll just pat your back instead!"

Edwith gulped down a mouthful in a hurry but choked, spitting some out over Jessynta's tail.

Edwith bowed his head to Jessynta in apology.

She gave him a poke with her paw.

Brecky laughed. "I don't think she is very amused, Edwith. Try to keep your food to yourself please."

The boys hurried off home.

Their mother had prepared a meal for them, which they ate quickly while trying to tell her, in between mouthfuls, about their games and what Edwith had done.

"Slow down, boys. You'll choke eating so fast! Poor Edwith. That might teach him a valuable lesson though. He might be happier when he sees what I bought while you were gone." She showed them a few long, brass chains she had found in a store. "I figured if they wanted to wear something around their neck, the chains you bought wouldn't be long enough.

"Fantastic. They'll love them. Thanks, Mum," said Will.

After helping Mum clear away their dishes, Nat suggested going for a short walk. "It's still light out, and I don't feel tired."

"That'll be fine. I have some things to do, and I need to talk to Dad anyway. See you in a while."

Once outside, Nat said, "I really want to check on Edwith." Nat was delighted when Edwith was the first to answer their shell call.

Hallo there, Nathaniel, I am feeling so much better. Mother Skyla's soup has really helped, and you should see Rayvinith spouting flames. I will see if he can manage to talk to William.

Al . . . o .ow.re..ou?

"Hi, Rayvinith, you need to think more slowly. I can't understand you."

He has not quite settled yet from his game with the flames, said Jessynta. *I shall have to work more with him. Oh, wait a minute. Guess who is coming along the beach? It looks like Zarven. Sorry to cut this short, but I need to talk with him.* Her voice faded out.

Will's head drooped, and his eyes started watering. "I so wanted to talk to him."

Nat gave him a smile in sympathy. "Never mind, Will. You'll be able to have a long chat with him tomorrow. I wonder what Ven will think of him. I can't wait to see them all again. Let's go home."

<div align="center">~~~~~</div>

"I know you're in a hurry but at least wait until you've

finished eating," shouted their mum as they raced off the next morning with pieces of toast still in their hands.

The dragons were waiting outside the cave as the brothers sprinted into the sunlight. Edwith ran toward them and tripped over Rayvinith's foot. The fire dragon was so startled that he narrowly missed setting Edwith's tail alight.

Watch it, scolded Edwith.

You watch it yourself.

A little angrily, Jessynta tried to restore calm. *Now then, you two. You have to control yourselves or you will end up hurting each other.*

The girls grinned at this exchange. "Something tells me that our dragon friends are pleased to see you again," said Brecky.

"So how long has it been for you this time? Only one night for us," said Pete.

Brecky looked at Izzy. "Just two days, but a lot has happened. Jessynta said she was talking to you with the shells when Ven appeared. Oh, wait up, he can tell you himself. Here he comes now."

"There you are. Great to see you again. You lucky devils. You've got another dragon. Wish I could meet one. I've been searching around the other side of the headland, and I found some more caves, so perhaps I'll find another egg."

Zarven, there might be a chance for you soon, said Jessynta. *Rayvinith's egg is not the last of the dragon eggs. Maybe one more near here.*

Ven's eyes nearly popped out of his head when he heard that. "You're not kidding me?" He jumped up and down in delight. "When? Where is it? Can we go now?"

Patience, young man. I do not know when or where yet.

Reluctantly he calmed down, although his eyes were still shining with delight. "I've been looking around more caves and found a really interesting one which seems to go back a long way, but it was so dark in there, I couldn't get very far. There were boxes stacked everywhere. Come with me; the dragons can stay here. There wouldn't be room for them anyway. It's not far away."

"Lucky we all brought torches." Pete took it out of his pocket and switched it on.

Ven's eyes opened wide. "Amazing! How does it work? You'll have to show it to my father. He'll be very interested in how it's made. Perhaps he could copy it. He's good at making things," said Ven, "although sometimes he's better at taking them apart!"

"I don't think you have the raw materials needed to make a battery to power it." Pete shrugged off Ven's confused look. "I'll explain later. Let's go exploring."

Brecky touched Ven's arm. "You'll get used to their strange words and the things they show us. Their explanations don't always make sense either."

This was the first time the brothers had ventured this far along the beach. They stared past the cliffs to where they gradually sloped downward on the other side of the headland, leading to a very large, flat area of beach forming a cove. In the center of the cove was the wide estuary of the river Staria they had seen from the top of the cliff near the girls' farm. A low, stone bridge spanned the river a little way beyond the cove, and there were many stone houses on either side of the river.

"That's my house over there." Ven pointed to a gray, stone house on the other side of the river. Next to it, a smaller building with a large chimney stood dark against the light gray of the house.

Will shielded his eyes and strained to see what Ven was talking about. "What is that big chimney set apart from the house?"

"That is my father's forge. He makes things in metal: horseshoes, of course, but also gates and all kinds of inventions. He's very clever, and he's teaching me as well. He says I have quite a knack for it." Ven smiled broadly.

Will looked at him with admiration.

Ven pointed to a nearby opening in the cliff. "This the cave I was telling you about."

Everyone followed him inside. Pete and Nat switched on their torches.

"Climb over those fallen rocks and see what I found," said Ven.

On the other side of the rocks, large containers practically filled the space. One had fallen on its side, revealing more wires and a large, smooth, flat surface.

"Is that what I think it is, Pete?" asked Will. "It looks very much like an old solar panel."

Nat chuckled. "That's a bit of wishful thinking. It's so covered with dirt and grit, there's no way you can tell what it is."

"What's a solar panel?" asked Lanya.

"It's a way to capture energy from the sun and store it until it's needed to run other machines," explained Pete. "But as I said, Will is just being imaginative. And even if it is, there's no way it could work."

"Maybe magic?" said Will hopefully. "Jessynta keeps saying she has magic."

"We better not touch it, as it might fall to pieces."

"Why don't you all come and meet my parents now?" Ven said. "You could see some of the things Father has invented."

"I think that we'll have to wait until another day to meet them. We should get back to the dragons. Our mother got presents for them," explained Pete.

As they neared the caves, Edwith bounded up to them full of delight once again, landing in front of Nat with a full somersault, making everyone clap at his acrobatic feat.

"Well done, and you didn't fall over doing it!" said Nat as he patted him on his side. "Just don't do it too often."

Pete opened his backpack. "Here's a surprise for being so good. Our mother went shopping and got these for you."

When the dragons saw the long brass chains, Edwith excitedly thumped his tail up and down. Rayvinith blew a tiny flame in the air, being careful not to aim it at anyone. Jessynta bowed her head in appreciation.

They shared them around, much to Pete's delight. "I'm really happy that you're able to share these without arguments. Very grown up of you."

Izzy was impressed too and smiled broadly at her sisters. "I think they're learning. Edwith, in particular, has come a long way. Rayvinith has also learned a great deal in the last two days. Haven't you?" she asked the young dragon, who preened his bright red feathers at her praise.

Jessynta searched her memories again and shared a great deal with me. I understand so much more about my abilities now. I admit to still feeling a little apprehensive, but she has promised to help me as much as she can, Rayvinith said.

Will patted Jessynta's wing. "Thank you so much for helping him."

Pete suddenly remembered the map they had found. "Before we came down to the beach, we had a look at the things the girls' father had unearthed and found a picture of what this world might have looked like hundreds of years ago. Do you have any memories of the land in the old times, Jessynta?"

Actually there is a big gap in my historical memories because of several things which happened in the past. Dragons were banished from human lands.

Pete raised his hand in surprise. "You were banished? Why?"

You will have to wait for another time, as it is quite another story altogether.

He folded his arms in disappointment.

I do not have memories of the past like Jessynta describes, so I cannot help. Maybe it is because I am not descended from a royal line like Jessynta, said Edwith.

You may well have something there. Our historical memories might be restricted to queens.

That is a pity, but it does not really matter. You can do all the remembering for us. Now that I am feeling better, I am ashamed of the way I behaved the other day. I will try hard to improve.

To prove it, he leaped into the air, misjudging the distance, and tripped over his tail.

Well, I cannot be too good, or you will not have anyone to entertain you.

CHAPTER FOURTEEN

NAT CRAMMED A LAST piece of toast in his mouth. "I was happy to see Edwith was getting over his stomach upset yesterday. He'll probably be completely recovered when we see him today. Wonder what mischief he has been up to since then. Come on, you two slowpokes. Let's get going."

Dragging his brothers up the hill to the cave portal, Nat could hardly wait to pull the fronds apart.

As soon as they stepped onto the sand, they were met by the dragons and the girls. The dragons all started to talk at once.

"Please slow down," said Nat. "When you all talk at once, it makes my head ache."

Edwith bounced around in excitement. *Just look how much I have grown. I must be twice as big.*

He was so excited to see you again, I had to restrain him from trying to climb the steps. He would probably have broken them, had I not. Edwith, try not to knock Nat over.

Rayvinith shyly touched Will with his wing. *I have grown too, and you should see how far I am able to shoot my flames now.*

Brecky grinned at the boys. "You can see how well they're all doing. Jessynta has had them practicing their exercises to strengthen their wings every day. In fact, I think we can try to ride them very soon now. Lanya is so good at making saddles. She's been working on them constantly with the help of our groom."

Will looked downcast. "Oh dear! I didn't think it would be this soon."

"Yes, I know you don't like the idea, but it's going to happen. Nat is excited. What about you, Pete?"

Pete nodded. "I'm quite eager to try, but I did tell Will it might be a while. Surely the dragons aren't ready yet. We haven't told our mother about the possibility, and our father still doesn't know any of you even exist!"

"I'm really looking forward to flying," said Lanya. "Though if we get many more dragons being born, we'll have to set up a business and employ helpers from the village! We brought the saddles down to the beach with us today. Let's try them out and see how many more alterations we shall have to make."

Will's mouth dropped open. "Today?"

Nat shook his finger at Will. "Don't be a scaredy cat."

"Nat, don't tease him. Don't worry, Will. It's only to try them on the dragons for a fitting. We left them at the path. Brecky and Izzy, can you help me with them please?"

The girls carried back what resembled overlarge horse saddles and reins combined. The big difference was the much longer girth straps and what looked like a cross between stirrups and calf length boots.

Lanya put one on Jessynta. "I've made it with two seating places."

"Why?" Nat examined the saddle.

"There are two bond mates for each dragon, aren't there?"

Pete said, "That makes sense. Will, you won't be so scared when Lanya is there with you." He gave Will a pat on the back. "So buck up."

"It would better if only Lanya rode on Rayvinith." Will's head drooped.

Rayvinith nudged Will with the tip of his wing again. *Do not worry! I will look after you, always supposing I can get off the ground. I certainly am not going very high. I am still working on my flaming, so I am not in a hurry either.*

Pete went closer to Jessynta for a better look. "How does it feel, Jessynta? Now that it's on, it doesn't look so complicated. These straps go underneath just like the pony's saddle. Does it feel tight?"

Lanya pointed at the saddle and the straps hanging from its side. "There's an extra strap fastening with stirrup boots from the saddles themselves to help hold each passenger on. That way they can't fall off."

I would never let any of you fall off. I will put a magic holding spell on you.

Brecky raised her hands and opened her eyes wide. "You can do that?"

I have always told you I have magic.

"Just to be on the safe side, I think we'll make a belt each, with straps to secure to the saddle." Lanya stepped back with her hands on her hips to admire her work. "How does it feel to you?" she asked Jessynta.

It feels nice and light, but we will have to go for a ride first to try it out. Flying comes naturally to us, but we need to strengthen our muscles. I fly differently, because I have to use magic to get in the air instead of using my wings so much. I have been trying this over the last week.

Brecky patted Jessynta's side. "You'll see. I watched her raising herself. It looks as though she's swimming through the air with only an occasional wing flap. Those little frills on her side seem to help her too."

Edwith was the next one to get his test saddle. Lanya had made this one to fit just behind Edwith's last head spike and in front of his wings. As his girth was quite a lot larger than Jessynta's middle, the securing straps had to be a lot longer.

His saddle had two to each seat to make it more secure.

You might have to watch your weight, Edwith, remarked Rayvinith cheekily.

Now do not start on me, you young whippersnapper. Edwith poked him with a claw.

"Actually, I agree, don't tease him," said Izzy. "Edwith has been behaving very nicely for the last day or two since his tummy upset. We have a lot of leather, and we'll have to make adjustments continually as you are all going to grow for quite a while longer."

Last of all, it was Rayvinith's turn to be fitted. After several small changes, the girls professed themselves satisfied.

It feels quite comfortable, and I am looking forward to trying to fly with William and Guillanya. I understand that scares you, William, but you need not worry. I shall be extremely careful. He moved forward to reassure William with a nuzzle.

Will responded to the young dragon by rubbing his snout. "Thank you, Rayvinith, and I love you to bits. I'll try to look forward to it." He took a deep breath and straightened his shoulders.

Brecky gave Rayvinith a stern look. "You're not going to have passengers for a while yet, as you have to get stronger. Edwith is the only one who has actually taken off and moved any distance and that was downhill. What you're going to do is practice flapping your wings up and down and see how it feels. For now, practice over the water's edge."

Edwith made a noise in his throat which sounded like a groan. *Ugh, I really do not like the sea. It has scary waves, but I really want to fly, so I shall be brave.* He flapped his wings.

Nat patted Edwith's side, all he could reach as the dragon was getting quite tall. "Way to go. Atta boy!" He gave him a thumbs up.

Jessynta stood up very straight and rotated her wings. *Peter and Brecchettya can ride on me in the sea, and we can get used to moving with my saddle.*

Pete noticed the frills on her sides. "Look! Those little structures on her sides are waving up and down like little sea ripples."

Brecky admired Jessynta's body. "She really does look graceful. I believe she's almost floating in the air."

That is the magic beginning to work on me. I shall soon be ready to fly.

Edwith jumped up and down eagerly. *So shall I.* He tipped over on landing. *Oops, I shall soon get the hang of it.*

Brecky shook a warning finger at them. "I think it will be a while yet for Edwith and Rayvinith to have riders, even while walking along the edge of the sea. Only Jessynta is really strong enough to bear weight, and of course, it's easier with the water helping her too. We rode on her back in the sea when we found Edwith, so we know she can bear us. I suggest that Pete and I get on her back, and she goes very slowly, keeping in the shallows. The other dragons can wear their saddles and walk slowly as well, while you four keep your eyes on the fastenings."

Edwith tilted his head to one side and looked at the sea. *Maybe I will jump up and down on the edge to see what it feels like.* He cautiously put one paw into the sea but jumped back when a wave broke over it. Losing his balance, he fell over. *Whoops! This will take some getting used to.* He gazed intently at the rippling waves. *The water does not feel too bad. This could be fun after all.*

Even Rayvinith tested the water with a paw.

"Right, Pete, let's mount up. Can you help us to get fastened in please, Izzy and Lanya? We'll put the belts on."

Pete studied the saddle in front of him and placed his foot into the booted stirrups to lift himself up. It took a little time to get everything fastened.

When Brecky and Pete were settled, he gave a thumbs up to the assembled group. "Ready, Jessynta? Then off we go."

She set off along the edge of the waves as Pete and Brecky cheered with delight.

Edwith trotted behind them at the water's edge. *Whoopee! This is fun. I can jump really high up in the air. Even if I come down unexpectedly, it does not hurt.* He proceeded to splash everybody within reach as he jumped up and down over the waves, landing upside down every so often and swallowing salty water by the gallons. As usual, his clowning around had everybody laughing until they almost cried.

Lanya was breathless from laughing when they made their way back to the sand. "Let's take off the saddles and get them dried. They're going to get spoiled from all the seawater if we don't. Edwith, I know you're now enjoying the sea, but it took me ages to make those saddles. When you want to frolic in the water, do it without the saddle."

They put the saddles on the sand and wiped them as dry as they could. "Lucky it's so sunny. We'll soon get dry as well," said Izzy.

Nat stroked Edwith's back as he lay on the warm sand. "Have you seen Ven lately?"

"Don't look now, but I think that's him." Izzy pointed at the figure running toward them.

He gasped heavily. "I'm glad to see you all. I found something strange in another of those caves around the headland. Follow me. Quickly as you can. The dragons better stay behind. The cave is quite small."

Ven led them to a cave at the base of the cliff. It was almost hidden by vegetation and overhanging branches of a fruit tree.

"Come in. Look over there at the back." He pointed to a small shelf of rock a little above his waist. On the shelf, an oval shaped object faintly glowed.

"I could swear that when I was here the other day, I saw it move," said Ven.

A shriek sounded from beside the shelf. "Aaahh help! Help! I'm falling!"

Pete rushed forward just in time to catch someone before they crashed to the floor of the cave. Peering closer at the person, Pete cried out, "I don't believe it! Cousin Zara!? How on earth did you get here? I'm absolutely gob smacked!"

"Pete! But it can't possibly be you! What's happening? I was just looking at a strange tree in my garden when I fell down a hole and into a tunnel. I felt like Alice in Wonderland, and I thought I must be dreaming."

"You're not dreaming, but I'm not sure how you got here."

Will and Nat rushed forward to greet their cousin. "Are you okay?" Will asked.

"Does this mean there's a portal in America too?" asked Nat.

"Portal? What are you talking about?" Zara glanced around the dark cave.

"I don't understand you being here either. Come outside the cave and into the light so we can see properly." Pete took her hand and led her outside. The others followed.

As soon as she saw the sea in front of her, Zara flopped down heavily on the nearest rock and rubbed her eyes. "W..w.. what's . . . h . . . h . . . happening? The sky is a funny greenish color." She reached out again and grabbed hold of Pete. "Pinch me."

He complied.

"Ouch! Then I'm not dreaming."

"Pete, who is this? Why is she coming from this cave and not the same cave you came from?" Lanya asked.

Zara looked between Pete and the others. "Who are these kids? What is she saying?"

"You aren't dreaming, and I'll try to explain." He hesitated when he realized that the Avalanyans were all staring dumbly, with bewildered expressions on their faces.

"Nat and Will, talk to Zara while I talk to Ven and the girls. They obviously can't understand her. One of them will have to mind meld with Zara. Explanations must wait until we can all understand each other."

Nat looked at Zara and was the first to find his voice.

"However did you get here? Talk about magic, this beats the lot!" Zara opened her mouth to speak, but quickly Nat continued. "Don't say another word. You won't believe this, but we are in an alternate universe. We got here a while ago, and things are indeed strange." He gestured dramatically at the Avalayans.

"These kids live here, and they don't speak our language! Welcome to Avalanya, Zara. I'll have to explain how we got here later." He put an arm around her shoulders to reassure her. "First you have to be given the ability to understand their language. It's easy."

Zara eyes sprang wide open. She shook her hands wildly, trying to shove him away. "What do you mean? Give me the ability?"

Nat frowned. "Don't look at me like that. By putting their hands on our temples, they can meld their minds with ours, and we all understand each other. You must have watched sci-fi movies. It's a bit like that."

Zara pushed him away angrily. "You're talking nonsense."

"You'll see. They have this magic way of uniting their minds with ours, and that lets us understand them. It sounds strange but it really does work. All you feel is a strange tingling and a jumble of words and sounds, which after a few minutes turns into language. Then, presto! We can understand each other. They call it mind melding. Please believe me. I'm not making this up."

Zara folded her arms and turned her back on him. "Ha! A likely story indeed. You must think I'm crazy. You're having me on. I won't fall for it."

While Nat was trying to reassure Zara, Pete had moved to their Avalanyan friends.

He pointed back in Zara's direction. "She's Zara. She's our cousin, but she lives in another part of our world miles and miles away from our home. I haven't got a clue how she got here, but here she is and will need to mind meld with one of you."

Brecky stepped forward. "By now we should be used to unexpected happenings. I don't think I can do a mind meld as it wasn't very long ago that I did one with you. Some people can do more than one, but I never have. I'd have to wait and see." She turned to Ven. "Could you do it, Ven?"

Ven shrugged. "Suppose so. Life is never dull with you lot. Better explain to her what I'll be doing then."

Pete returned to Zara, took hold of her hands and repeated what Nat had said to her. Then he gestured for Ven to come over. "This is Ven. The girls are his cousins. We've all done this mind meld thing. Just relax and let it happen. Trust me. You'll be okay."

"Do I have to?" Zara pulled a face, still looking anxiously at Pete.

"Only if you want to figure out how you got here." Pete waited patiently.

Finally, Zara stood up and allowed Ven to approach her. She shrank back a little from him as he gently put his hands on the sides of her head. "Oh, what now?"

She jumped as she heard Ven's voice in her mind.

It really is all right. I won't hurt you. The others all did this too, and it makes everything so much easier. Please relax and trust me.

His voice in her head and the tingling sensation made her shiver, but a look of encouragement from Pete reassured her.

After a few seconds, Ven dropped his hands and said out loud, "Hi, Zara. Sorry about all that. I'm Ven, and these are my cousins: Brecky, Izzy, and Lanya."

Zara's eyes nearly popped out of her head. "A-maz-ing. I can understand you perfectly, but I would never have believed anything like this could happen. I was just out exploring in the garden when—"

Stopping in mid-sentence, she squealed, looking wildly around her. "Who's talking now? Your lips aren't moving. Are you in my head again?" Her legs gave way, and she fell to the ground.

Ven nearly lost his balance too. "It's coming from the egg! There's something inside. It's a dragon! At last! My turn! I'm coming!

Zara! Zarven! Please help me get out. It is so dark in here, and it is so cramped. I want so much to get born, and I need you both.

Ven shouted in delight, "You must be hatching!"

He turned excitedly to Zara, his eyes shining. "Zara, get up! Follow me quickly. No time to explain. We're needed." He grabbed hold of her hand to pull her into the cave.

Nat jumped up and down with excitement. "Look at their faces. Three guesses what has just happened!"

Will grinned broadly. "Hooray, it's a new dragon egg! Look, here come the other dragons."

Ven and Zara rushed pell-mell back into the cave, nearly falling over each other in their eagerness.

"What is it and who's talking?" asked Zara.

Ven pointed to the oval-shaped thing rocking madly on the shelf.

It is I, Crystalya. I am an earth dragon, or I will be if I can get out of this wretched shell. Come over here and help me. I have pierced it with my egg tooth, but I cannot get the pieces of shell out of the way.

"Come on, Zara. She's calling to us from inside her egg. I've been waiting ages for this moment. It's a dragon!" He turned the egg until he found the crack.

Zara was confused but obediently began pulling at the shell.

Pete and the other children squeezed into the cave behind them. "Eureka! Just look at that." They all stared at the egg.

"Ven! Zara! Make room; we're ready to help!" Pete said as they joined Ven and Zara. "This is getting to be a habit. If this goes on, I shall be able to advertise myself as a midwife or mid-husband to dragon babies!" said Pete.

They all pulled until, at last, out came a tiny purple dragon.

Crystalya promptly wrapped herself around Ven and Zara so tightly, they could hardly breathe.

Zara cringed, and Ven had an expression of surprise on his face.

"I think they are bonding with the new dragon," Will said.

Zara grabbed her stomach. "Is there any food in this world? I'm so hungry it hurts."

"Me too," agreed Ven, looking around desperately. "Let's get out of here."

Zara and Ven managed to struggle out of the cave with the baby dragon still clinging to them.

At the sight of the three dragons, Zara almost passed out with fright. If Crystalya had not been wrapped around her, she would have fallen to the ground.

Do not be frightened of us. We are friends, just like your little baby one there, said Jessynta.

Zara looked from one to the other of the children. "Who said that?"

Jessynta bowed her head gently.

Zara sprang out of Crystalya's paws and looked at Pete for help.

"What is this blue creature? Is she the one who's talking to me?"

I am called Jessynta. Welcome, Zara and Crystalya. I am the queen of these dragons. We shall introduce ourselves properly in a few minutes, but for now, you must be hungry.

CRYSTALYA

CHAPTER FIFTEEN

ZARA STARED WIDE-EYED AT the three enormous dragons in front of her and at the beautiful purple dragon who had just hatched, her hunger temporarily forgotten.

She reached out her hands imploringly to Pete. "Help me? I just don't understand. Did the blue dragon in front of me just speak to me?" She dissolved into tears and sank down beside Crystalya.

Pete sat on the sand next to her. "I know this is a shock. I'll try to tell you what's happened. We are all in an alternate universe. We three boys were all called here several days ago by the dragons to help them hatch. It wasn't quite so sudden for us though. When we touched them as they hatched, we bonded to them. They don't have a spoken language, but they speak in our minds. You've heard of telepathy, haven't you?"

Zara nodded feebly as she wiped her eyes. "But are we now here forever?"

"Oh, no, not at all. We go home every night. We've been coming here for a while now, and we've become fast friends with the kids who live here. We helped these three dragons out of their shells together. They call this island Avalanya and made us all so welcome. We even met their mother. Her name is Skyla, and they met our mother as well."

"Aunt Rachel came here too? Really? Do you suppose my

mother could come here too?" Zara clasped her hands together in delight.

Before Pete could answer, Crystalya began to sob loudly.

Zara was beside herself. "Oh, my dear, how can we help you? Pete, tell me what to do for her."

Suddenly Zara clutched at her stomach. "W . . . w . . . why am I so h . . . hungry?" she stammered in pain. "I only had lunch a short while ago. Has anyone any food? Even a snack? I'm a wreck. I don't usually cry all over the place like this."

Ven rubbed his stomach. "I'm ravenous too."

Jessynta stepped forward, raising one of her front paws. *You must find food. Crystalya is hungry. Being bonded makes you feel their emotions. I shall lessen the bond for them as soon as I can but find food quickly, please. We will help, but you explain it to Zara. Do not cry, little Crystalya. I will go and get food immediately. You go look too, Edwith.*

Right, boss. I have meat I have been saving for a snack. I will get it. I will not let you starve, Crystalya!

I can stay here and keep you company, said Rayvinith. *Do not cry. The others will bring food soon.*

Zara looked with awe at the dragons as they left. "What about me?"

Pete produced his backpack. "I have snacks for you and Nat has too. We hardly ever go out without food."

Pete managed to squeeze past Crystalya to put an arm around Zara as he held out crisps, a few peanuts, and crackers. "While the dragons are searching, I'll tell you a little about what is happening to you."

Pete went on to explain how they discovered Avalanya, how they met the girls, and some of their adventures.

"Jessynta, the blue dragon, is bonded to me and Brecky." Pete gestured toward the dragon.

Brecky came closer. "I'm Brecky. We think each dragon gets two bond mates because you lot have to go home each night. This way, they're never alone."

"I'm Izzy. Nat and I are bonded with Edwith, the greenish white dragon."

"Yeaah! Watch out for our Edwith. He's a complete clown. Guaranteed to make you laugh, and if you're not careful, he can sometimes trip over you." Nat had a broad grin.

"Hi, Zara, pleased to meet you. I'm Lanya. Your cousin Will and I bonded with this lovely, feathery, red dragon called Rayvinith. He's learning to shoot fire, so don't get too close to him, or you might get accidentally scalded."

Zara shrunk away from Rayvinith and clung to Crystalya.

Pete looked at Lanya angrily. "Don't frighten Zara. I've only just reassured her."

Rayvinith shyly lowered his feathery head down to Zara's level. Please do not take any notice of Lanya. I did have some trouble at first controlling my flames, but I am learning fast, am I not, Lanya?

Lanya patted his back apologetically, and he purred in delight at her caress. "Zara, he really is a sweetie! If you can get a hand free from Crystalya for a moment, you can stroke the lovely red feathers on his paws."

Rayvinith gently extended a feathered paw, which Zara took courageously with a smile. "They really are very soft."

Jessynta appeared with a wriggling fish. *Edwith, stop crowding the poor young thing and get out of my way.*

Edwith tried to nudge Jessynta out of the way with his wing. *No, I was here first. Look, I have brought you some of my favorite meat.*

Crystalya timidly smelled their offerings and shuddered. Clinging even more tightly to Zara and Ven, she said, *I do not like any of that. I want something else. Ugh! I want . . .* but she couldn't tell them what she wanted.

They all looked puzzled. Pete, who was sitting watching with his brows furrowed in thought, sat up straight. His face suddenly brightened. "Hold on. Perhaps she's a vegetarian like us and doesn't eat meat and is not keen on fish. Why don't we look for fruit, nuts, grasses, and maybe small greenery? We could cut it up really small. Maybe she's like young birds whose mother regurgitates her own food for her chicks."

"Yuck!" exclaimed Zara, pulling a face and sticking out her tongue. "She's very cute, and I adore her, but I am absolutely not going to regurgitate my food for anyone."

The others all looked a little disgusted.

"We'll look around up there," Nat said. He and Will quickly climbed the hillside, which was not as steep as the cliffs on the other side of the headland. They picked fruit from the tree above them. Will spotted nuts on another tree and edible grasses. Ven rummaged in a bag he had with him for more fresh fruit.

In a few minutes, the children had collected quite a large selection of greenery and fruits. Pete grinned broadly and produced a small fork from his backpack. "Lucky I always carry all sorts of gear with me, as you never know what you will come across in this world." He mashed up the softest pieces of fruit he could find. "This will do instead of swallowing it ourselves first. I don't much like the idea of regurgitation either!"

Ven offered fruit out to the baby dragon, who sniffed at it. After daintily licking one piece of fruit with a long purple tongue, she began to gobble it down so fast, they were worried she would choke.

"Slow down, Crystalya. " Zara gently patted her back.

Eventually she settled down to eat a little more slowly, relinquishing her tight hold on Ven and Zara, although she kept an eye on them both.

While she was eating, Zara said to the boys, "This is still a mystery to me. We'd just moved into a new house, and I went exploring in the garden. There was a strange kind of tree, and as I got closer, I got tangled up in its branches. It was all round me, and its branches were shaking. My feet slipped from under me. I lost my balance and started to slide down a steep slope into a deep hole. It was so scary." She shivered at the memory. "Next thing I knew, Pete was there to catch me."

"That sounds a bit like what happened to me. I fell down a tunnel too and was really scared out of my wits. I met the girls, then Jessynta called us from inside her egg."

Ven frowned. "I still need to eat something. I gave most of the food in my pack to Crystalya."

"Why don't you eat the fish that Jesssynta brought? We don't want to waste it. Jesssynta, could you cook it for him please?" We live closest I'll run back home for more food." Izzy ran off around the headland.

While Izzy was gone, the boys sat down on the sandy beach around the little dragon. Jessynta touched Ven and Zara gently with her wing.

Zarven, Zara, please put your hands here on my chest, and I will lessen your bonds a little so you will not feel Crystalya's emotions so strongly.

They looked a little puzzled but did as she asked.

There! Do you feel a little better now?

Zara and Ven had trembled a bit as they touched her, but after a few minutes, both grinned at each other.

"Much better now," said Zara.

Ven looked at Crystalya. "Looks like you've finished eating. Are you feeling better now?"

I am feeling so much better now that I have eaten, so I will just rest here in this lovely warm sun, but you will not go anywhere, will you? She insisted on resting her head on Zara's lap and clasping Ven with a soft forepaw at the same time.

"Here comes Izzy with more food," said Ven.

Rayvinith, I will bring extra for you so you can stay here if you like. However, I am still hungry. Edwith hopped off gaily down the beach.

Now that is really thoughtful of you, my friend. Rayvinith tipped his wing to Edwith in thanks.

Jessynta was finishing the fish that Ven hadn't eaten, but her jaw dropped in surprise at his words. *That is amazingly good of Edwith. I would never have thought he could be so caring. He is maturing. Do make sure to praise him when he returns.*

Everyone nodded, especially Izzy.

When Edwith returned to give Rayvinith scraps of meat, she and Nat smiled with pride and gave him a large hug. He responded by trying to thump his spiked tail, showering Izzy and Nat with sand.

Oops! Hope that did not get in your eyes.

They laughed at him and brushed themselves down.

Now that Crystalya was content, everyone began asking questions.

Pete said, "We still don't understand how it is that you, living in Virginia, can possibly be here with us, when our access was from a cave in England."

Jessynta looked up. *There are many portals to enter our world, and Zara was obviously called here by Crystalya. You are related to each other, so there may be something in that too.*

Crystalya batted her long purple eyelashes demurely. *Yes, I wanted you, so I called very loudly, a portal opened, and you found me. I needed Zarven too.*

Young Crystalya, you should try to access your mother's memories that she would have given to you whilst you were in egg, said Jessynta.

"We're continually being flabbergasted by new revelations. So much has happened that I hardly know where I am anymore," said Pete.

Brecky giggled and poked him. "You are here in Avalanya! But we'd better collect Crystalya's shell pieces before we forget. We'll need to find a cave for Crystalya."

At the sound of her name, Crystalya stood, stretched, and unfurled her wings.

Zara squealed in surprise. "Just look at Crystalya! She isn't pale purple anymore. Look at her silver eyes and her wings. She is unbelievably gorgeous."

They looked over in amazement. She had deepened her color to a sparkling purple. All over her body, her scales glittered like gems, particularly around her head and claws. The struts of her wings were studded with amethysts and crystals. "I can't believe it. Just look! Did you ever see such a beautiful sight?" said Zara, staring at the dragon with wide eyes.

The stunned kids gazed in silent awe at her beautiful wings as she flapped them gently up and down, making the gems sparkle in the sunlight.

Crystalya is a dragon of the earth, so she displays the minerals of the earth. Her magic is affecting us as well. Jessynta stretched to her full length.

Pete gave a surprised gasp at Jessynta. "Look at her. She's sparkling like the ocean on a brilliant sunny day."

The other dragons preened themselves. It seemed that with Crystalya's coming, they, too, were more beautiful.

Nat and Izzy looked at each other in delight as they saw Edwith bright and gleaming with all the colors of the rainbow.

Rayvinith raised his feathered wings as high as he was able and ruffled them proudly. He looked as though he was on fire in the sunlight.

Pete and Brecky tore themselves away from the splendid sight of Jessynta to collect the pieces of shell from the cave. Brecky put them in a bag for Zara. "Know that these shell pieces are very special. They have magic properties."

"What do you mean?"

"We use them to talk to our dragons when we get home," explained Will.

"I might have known. I'll never get used to this." She sighed. "I'm suffering from overload!"

Crystalya, who had been posing rather dramatically,

stopped, lowered her fantastic wings, and looked at Brecky. *Did you say something about a cave for me? I cannot sleep in a cave. By myself? Nobody with me? Can I not sleep with Zara or Zarven?*

Jessynta moved closer and raised a wing to cover her. *Little one, we each have chosen big caves for ourselves. But until we find one for you, I shall look after you. I can shelter you in my cave.*

Crystalya looked up at her from under her purple lashes. *Yes, that sounds good. You can tell me more of what I need to know. I am very beautiful, but I have a lot to learn in my new life.*

Ven and Zara gazed at her in pride.

"I've got a tremendous idea," said Will. "Now that Zara has joined us from her home in the US, we can all go back with her. We could pay a surprise visit to her family."

Jessynta raised her head and shook one of her paws at him. *Not so. You can only depart through the portal you used to enter Avalanya. I fear it would cause an anomaly, because it is impossible to travel within your world like that. If Zara happened to be visiting your house, she would then be able to come here using the same portal you use.*

Will looked disappointed but sadly nodded his head. "But it would have been fun if we could have done it!"

Pete smiled happily at Zara. "When you get home, we can do a video chat about these new adventures, and Aunt Anita can talk to Mum."

Crystalya lifted her head. *What do you mean? Is Zara going somewhere?*

Pete patted Crystalya's head. "This is a tricky one. Not only do we four live in a different world, but Zara even lives in a different part of our world than we do. She lives so far away from us that her time is a bit different to ours. Oh dear, this is very complicated." He threw up his hands in despair.

Jessynta touched Pete gently with her wing. *Do not concern yourself too much with this. I know all about your time differences. They used to have them in our world too. I shall help Crystalya work it out, and I shall always know when one of you is about to arrive.*

Zara frowned. "You seem to be in charge of the dragons, and you have all the answers. Why is that?"

I am the leader in the events my mother initiated by hiding the eggs in parts of the world of Avalanya before its final devastation. She was the sovereign queen of that world, and I am her sole descendent. Not all has been revealed to me, and there is much more still unanswered. It is going to take a great deal of work on my part.

Jessynta continued with a question of her own. *What is this video call you talked about? Is it like scrying?*

Pete tilted his head. "I'm not sure how to explain it to you. I'm not a computer expert like our father. We have these objects we call satellites circling our world, and we get information from them. It's all powered by electricity of some kind or another. The whole thing is like an invisible, giant spiderweb that stretches over the entire world. When it first came out, it was even referred to as the worldwide web. Everyone gets connected to it. We can send messages through it or even use it to talk with our devices."

Will looked excited and broke in, eager to show off his knowledge. "We call our devices computers, and there are all types, some big and some very small. We use a small one called a tablet. Everybody has a number, and when we tap our name or number on a keyboard, it connects us. There's a little camera inside which photographs us and a glass screen we look at. When we tap in the person's special number, they appear on the screen as well! They see us too. Smart phones do the same thing."

Nat shook his head at his brother. "Take a breath, Will, for heaven's sake. Good luck if any of you lot can understand all that."

The Avalanyans merely shrugged their shoulders and

looked bewildered. Brecky gestured to Ven as if washing her hands. "They talk about stuff like this all the time."

Jessynta tapped a claw on the ground and lowered her head to look at the marks she had made. *That sounds interesting. A bit like some kind of magic. Actually, I believe there was something similar to your satellites in use in our world before the fall, and there may even be some left up in the sky. I should not think any of them still work. They did use sun power, although that knowledge is lost. Next time you come, will you bring one or even two of these tablets with you?*

Pete looked thoughtful and scratched his head. "Certainly, but they won't be any use to you. They won't work."

You never know what I can do with my magic.

Pete stared at her. "That might be beyond even you, but we have to leave that discussion for another time. I hate to break things up, but we must leave. However, as Zara lives in a different place from us, she may be able to stay a little longer and get to talk with you."

"Oh no, are you going to leave me here alone?" asked Zara.

"You have Crystalya, Ven, and the girls," said Pete.

Crystalya began crying again. *You are talking about leaving. What is happening now?*

Ven soothed her while Jessynta sheltered her and Zara with a comforting wing. *I know it is hard, but after they leave, I will explain more to you and Zara.*

Brecky put her arm around Zara. "We can help you to settle, and I'll get our mother to come down to the beach to meet you. You'll like her."

Pete smiled at her encouragingly. "You and Ven can introduce Crystalya to her. I know this is hard to understand, but it's all part of coming to this extraordinary world. After all, if you hadn't come here, you would never have met your beautiful Crystalya. Your parents are going to have a really hard time believing you too. Our father has been away, so he doesn't even know yet. Be sure to video call as soon as you get home. We can help explain it to them."

"I can't wait for my parents to meet our beautiful Crystalya. Oh, but wait a minute, my mum and dad are never going to be able to survive that fall. I'm actually wondering myself about climbing up again. Let's go look at the cave." She grabbed Pete's arm.

Pete frowned and looked at his brothers. "What do you think? I'm sure we have enough time left, and we should see the place. It all happened so fast; I didn't really take much notice."

"Sure. You're the one who always seems to know when we should go home anyway. Do you have your torch with you? We'll probably need it." Nat pulled Will after him to Zara's cave.

Zara gave Crystalya a hug. "You stay here, and Ven will look after you."

"Your farm workers built those steps for our cave. Why don't you come with us and see what you think? Maybe you could ask them to help again," Pete said to Brecky.

"That's a good idea. Lanya can come too and leave Izzy with Ven."

Zara led them to the cave where Nat and Will were waiting.

Pete switched on his torch. "Look, there's the shelf where the egg was. Just above and to the side of it is a dark hole." Pete pointed his torch into the opening.

"Nat, give me a hand up so I can reach it from the shelf." Zara scrambled onto the ledge and peered inside the hole. "I can see branches. I'll go inside." She climbed onto a branch and moved smaller twigs out of the way.

She squealed in surprise. "I can see daylight now, but a huge tree trunk is blocking the way." Tears welled in her eyes. "I won't be able to go home."

Pete ran his fingers through his hair as he thought.

Will pushed past Pete. "These portals are magic. They'll

only open for the one who first comes through. We have to wait until it senses that Zara is alone."

"You're going to leave me here alone?" she screamed.

"Trust me, Zara. We'll just go to the cave entrance. You reach up and touch that tree trunk." Will gestured for everyone to step back.

Zara, Will is correct. That is what must happen. When they get outside the cave, the portal will open for you, said Jessynta from outside the cave. *Peek through and you will see your garden.*

Pete called from outside the cave, "Do as she says, but don't stay there. Come right back. Call out when you're on the shelf, and I'll help you down."

Zara did as she was told. "It worked! It was just as Jessynta said. It opened. Come and help me down."

Everyone crowded back into the cave and clapped in relief when they saw her standing there with a huge grin of relief.

"I was so scared when you left, but wasn't I brave? I did it!" She went around hugging everybody with tears of joy.

Brecky touched her arm again. "No need to worry about that shelf. I'll get our workmen to build something."

"Now that's all sorted, we really must go home. You'll be fine now. See you on a video call later, Zara," Pete said.

The brothers said goodbye to everyone and left for the other side of the promontory and their cave.

When they emerged into their world, they discovered that more time had gone by than usual, and they were extremely hungry.

"It's a good thing Mum knows about all this. Remember to keep quiet about the saddles and flying for a while yet. That could make her a little anxious. Wonder if she's waiting for us," said Nat as they went inside the house.

He needn't have worried, as she was busy making dinner.

"Hi, Mum! You'll never guess what happened in Avalanya today," said Will.

CHAPTER SIXTEEN

"WHAT'S HAPPENED NOW? SOMETHING momentous, judging by the look on your faces. You'd better sit down and tell me all about it. Food can wait! I'll get us all a drink." Their mother took juice out of the fridge and sat down at the kitchen table. "I'm all ears."

"We'd only just arrived and—"

"Ven came rushing up—"

"He said he'd found something in a cave—"

"We left the dragons and ran after him—"

Rachel spread her hands wide apart with a cut off motion. "Stop! Stop! I can't understand a word when you all talk at once. Start over. Pete, you begin."

"Ven said to leave the dragons, because he'd found something in a cave which was too small for them all to get in."

Nat tapped his foot impatiently and couldn't wait for his turn. "When we got to the cave—"

Pete pushed him away. "No. I'm telling it. I got there first, and this girl dropped out of a large opening inside the cave, and I caught her! It was cousin Zara!"

"You mean Anita's girl? But they moved to the US several weeks ago. They can't be back already." She shook her head in bewilderment.

"I know. We couldn't believe it either," said Pete. "She came through a new portal, all the way from the States."

"Pete, do get on with the story. Ven had found another dragon egg about to hatch, and it wanted Ven and Zara as bond mates," said Will eagerly.

Nat poked Will. "Let him finish."

"The most beautiful dragon hatched. She's purple, and her eyes are silver. Her name is Crystalya, but get this, Mum! When she opened her wings, the struts were crusted with amethysts and crystals like the inside of that geode you've got at home. You know the one I mean? That huge amethyst one everybody always admires. You're going to love her. Ven and Zara are already completely besotted. They can't take their eyes off her."

Will finally managed to get a word in. "We're going to video chat with Zara later, and you'll have to talk to Aunt Anita and Uncle Mark as well."

"I'm almost too excited about all this to eat," said Nat. "With their time difference, Zara might not have left Avalanya yet."

Their mother slowly got up and mechanically began to serve up their meal. "I'll say this for our holiday—there's never a moment to get bored. However are we going to tell Dad all that has happened now? Oh dear! The mind boggles." She cradled her chin in her hands and sighed.

"Oh yes, I almost forgot. While you were gone, Dad phoned. His work has finished, and he's coming home tomorrow. No more work. He'll be here for the rest of our rental agreement."

Nat exclaimed, "Oh! I forgot we'll have to go home. Whatever are we going to do?" He looked at his brothers with a worried expression, and his shoulders slumped.

Pete, however, sat up straight. "I don't believe Jessynta will let us lose contact after all the trouble she went to in the beginning. She'll have a solution."

Will scratched his head. "Zara just came through a new portal, didn't she? That must mean there are others. Jessynta will find us one close to our home." He grinned triumphantly. "There! I've solved it."

Pete laughed at the proud expression on his face. "Yes, that's a possibility. Let's eat up first. Then we'll tell Mum more about today. Keep an eye on the time, then we can talk to Zara."

When they finally managed to contact Zara and her parents, she too was very eager to talk about her day.

Her parents were completely bewildered. They hadn't believed Zara's incredible tale at all. Seeing how confused Zara's parents were, Rachel tapped Pete's shoulder.

"This is too difficult when everyone tries to talk at once. Why don't I go upstairs to my room and talk calmly to my sister and Mark on my tablet without you lot. Then you can talk on your own."

"Good idea, Mum," said Pete.

When everyone was settled, Pete got a chance to talk. "So, Zara, what happened after we left? The whole thing was so overwhelming, I could hardly think straight when we got home."

"You were feeling like that? Can you even begin to realize how confusing I found everything? What with all that stuff about the mind melding, dragons, and kids from another world. I'm already beginning to wonder if I shall soon wake up and find that this has all been a very vivid dream. The only way I know it wasn't is because I feel a faint presence of my Crystalya in my mind. Do you feel the dragons too?"

"Yes, we all do, and Jessynta says the connection will get stronger. But in the meantime, did she explain how you can talk to her from our world using those precious shell pieces?"

"Yes, she did, but Crystalya was very upset when I said I had to leave, so we didn't get very far with the explanation. Jessynta managed to explain things to her about all the dragons having two bond mates so they would be cared for when we were not there. Ven seems very nice too. Isn't it funny that he's also their cousin like you are mine?"

"Jessynta says that's probably how you were called into the circle. She seems to be so knowledgeable about our world, although she says she hasn't even remembered everything her mother left her yet. Wouldn't it be fun if your parents could come and meet ours in Avalanya? We could have a grand party!" Nat shook his hands in the air.

"Oh no. She told me that for some reason to do with some anomaly or other, there couldn't be too many earth people there at the same time. If both your parents are there, mine shouldn't be there at the same time. They'll be able to visit when you aren't there though. Jessynta seems so clever. Who knows, maybe she'll work something out one day."

"We'll definitely have to do some planning ahead then," said Pete. "We haven't told Dad yet. He'll be here tomorrow night. We'll tell him then and try to arrange a visit for him.'"

"I was a little frightened when you left me on Avalanya. However, the girls got their mother down to the beach to meet me and be introduced to our Crystalya. She just loved her. Ven and I are so proud of Crystalya, and Edwith is being very protective of her too. He's so funny; he started shaking the trees to bring down more fruit. Izzy wasn't too thrilled though. He made a huge one fall on her head!"

Nat laughed. "That sounds just typical of our Edwith and his tricks!"

"I have to admit, I'm concerned about going back on my own again. What if it won't work?"

"You have no need to worry about it," said Nat. "Pete will tell you that I worried about everything. I didn't think we would ever find our way back to Avalanya, but he said to trust Jessynta, and he was right."

Zara sighed. "Although you helped me with my portal, and the workmen will build steps, I'm still a little worried about it."

Pete said. "Ours was much easier after the workmen finished, but it might be a few days before your parents will be able to visit."

"Still, that will give us time to get our dad to visit," said Nat.

"And we'll finally get to meet Ven's parents. Brecky said he has to be there to do the mind meld with Dad."

"It will also give me time to get used to coming on my own anyway. Jessynta said she and the other dragons would all be there to help us."

"There you are then. Your time in Virginia is five hours behind our time zone, so let's meet in Avalanya tomorrow at eight in your morning. That will be about one in the afternoon for us. Tomorrow will be quite, quite mad!" said Pete with a huge grin.

After saying goodnight to Zara, the boys went to find their mother. "Mum, did you manage to convince Aunt Anita and Uncle Mark?" asked Nat.

"I'm not too sure. They're very doubtful and, of course, confused. They'll definitely have to see for themselves."

~~~~~

The next afternoon came at last, and the boys tore up the hill to the portal.

Only Jessynta and Brecky greeted them outside the cave.

Good morning, boys. Edwith and Rayvinith are hunting. Izchetttya and Guillanya are helping Zarven and Crystalya choose her new cave. She spent the night with Jessynta. They are now searching for a cave further down the beach, not too far from ours and very close to where Crystalya hatched. If you look in the direction of the promontory, you will probably be able to see them.

"There they are. Let's go meet them," said Will.

Where is my Zara? asked Crystalya. *Why is she not with you? Did you not bring her?*

"Didn't Jessynta explain that we earth kids live a long way from each other and don't come through the same portal?" said Nat.

Oh dear, this is so complicated. I will never sort it out. Tears fell from her eyes.
~~~~~

"Come now, dear," said Ven, patting her gently. "I'm here all the time. You'll get used to it."

I feel Zara coming very soon. Do you sense her yet, Crystalya? We can go meet her, said Jessynta.

Ooh, yes! She is coming! Zara, hurry up, hurry up. Crystalya rushed to the cave where they had first seen Zara arrive, almost knocking her over in excitement when she emerged.

"It worked! I made it! But I'll be glad when Skyla's workmen make some kind of steps. It's a high jump from that shelf. I'm happy to see you too, Crystalya." Zara hugged her tightly. "And you, Ven. Great to see everyone!"

Now we can have more fun and maybe another feast soon. Edwith bounced up the beach, followed closely by Rayvinith.

"Wait up, Edwith. We have something very important to talk about before we do anything else today," said Pete. "We're only staying in our holiday home for another few days of our time and will be going back to our home in London. It's ever so far away from here, so I don't see how we can keep coming through this portal. What can we do about it?"

Do not worry. I have been thinking about this for a while, Jessynta said. *Luckily, I have a solution from what you have told me about your devices. I believe that I can find a way for you to use your portable device to set up a new portal right where you live. Can you take images with your device? Do you have the exact location of your house?*

"Yes, we can take photos. Do you mean location in latitude and longitude?" Pete asked.

Ah, yes, latitude and longitude.

"Our tablets determine our exact latitude and longitude position by use of the satellites I told you about," said Pete. "It won't be of any use to you in your world. Do you really think you'll be able to use our technology?"

Yes, I do. I can use my magic to get your technology to work. I will move your portal. Did you bring any of those devices with you?

Will stood very straight and proudly said, "Didn't I tell you yesterday that Jessynta would sort it?"

However, Pete still looked worried. "Will and I both brought one to show you, but as I said, our tablets won't work here. If we try to use them, the battery will go dead like our phones did."

You were not listening to me. I use magic and all I need to do is to touch them. I am sure I will be able to get them to work.

"That's really something," said Nat. "I think our father will be very impressed. He works with computers all the time. He's coming to our holiday house tonight, and we will be telling him about all our adventures. We shall make him come with us tomorrow." Nat crossed his fingers.

"Be sure to explain to him all about the mind melding, and I'll tell my father too. He can meet you all and do the mind meld with him," said Ven.

"We'll tell him everything that has happened so far. Luckily our mother has been here, or we'd never convince him," said Will.

Pete frowned. "Jessynta, you told us it was normal for adults to feel very tired here because of the time anomaly. However, I've noticed that I'm beginning to feel more tired than when we began all this."

Oh no! I should have thought more about this, but everything is happening so fast. Each time something unusual happens, I have to delve into my memories more and more. I think we might have to strengthen our links. I really am devastated about all my mistakes. Please forgive my ignorance. She lowered her head to the ground.

After several minutes of silence, she settled herself on the sand and spoke again. *I will try it with you first, Peter. If it does what I think it will, the others can copy us. Come closer to me, so you can reach the scales closest to my heart. Lean as close to me as you are able with your chest and put your arms around me as far as you can. Then take a deep breath, hold it, and concentrate on me as much as possible. You might feel a slight pressure somewhere on your body, probably your arm, but it will not hurt. So just relax.*

Pete pursed his lips and looked apprehensive. Then he straightened his shoulders and moved close to the seated dragon. He hugged her tightly.

"Ooh!" He scratched his arm. "Will it leave a mark?"

Eventually there will be a little mark but not yet, said Jessynta.

Brecky had been watching. "Did that hurt, Pete?"

"No, I'm quite okay. It tickled a bit."

Jessynta raised her wing and waved it at Pete. *I need to talk privately with the dragons to explain how to accomplish the link.*

Nat nudged Will. "Another touchy-feely thing. We're always touching people in this world." He made a face at the girls.

Edwith gestured to Nat with a wingtip and sat down next to him. Rayvinith shyly extended a wingtip to Will.

Crystalya timidly crouched down closer to Zara. *Please look at me. Jessynta has explained it to me, and I know exactly how to make the link.*

"Do we have to do this?" asked Zara. "Everything is happening so fast."

I am hoping this will make your visits easier. You four will get a mark on one of your arms. It will be quite small and may take a couple of days to appear. It will only be visible to those who have bonded with a dragon.

"It doesn't hurt. Honest," Pete said.

Children, get as close as you can to your dragons, give them a big hug, and relax.

Zara and the others put their arms around their dragons. Zara made a small squeak but otherwise said she was feeling okay.

The dragons responded to all the hugging with obvious delight. Crystalya purred like a large cat. Edwith stood up and attempted a somersault, managing to shower them all with sand.

Enough of all this. Where is our feast? said Edwith, shaking himself free of sand.

"Don't you ever think about anything but food?" Izzy patted him gently.

We always eat when our friends come.

"He's right as usual," agreed Lanya. "Why don't we run up to our house to get snacks?"

"I'll come with you," said Izzy.

I did just hunt, but I put a few morsels in my cave. Edwith hopped off.

Pete turned to Jessynta. "What will this mark do for us?"

It should bind you more strongly to your dragons and cut down the time anomaly, so even if you do not come here for one or two days, it will not be as long as it was before.

"Don't we get the marks as well?" asked Brecky.

You live here so do not need them. Boys, once we get the tablets working here, they—together with your new marks—should make it possible for us to talk without the shells.

"That's useful, because we don't carry the shells everywhere," said Nat.

Izzy and Lanya returned with a few snacks, including fruit and cheese for Crystalya. Edwith shared scraps with Rayvinith, and they all settled down to rest in the sun.

Crystalya was delighted with the snacks the girls had brought for her and daintily licked up every morsel.

Jessynta stretched out on the sand. *Time to show me those tablets of yours.*

Pete took a tablet from his backpack and laid out a cloth to rest it on.

Edwith came closer to look.

"Edwith, you keep well away so sand doesn't get into it."

Pete opened it up and pointed to the screen and the keypad.

Jessynta watched him intently as he tapped on a key. Of course nothing happened, and the screen remained dark.

When she bent forward with an outstretched claw, he grabbed it. "You're too big to push the key down. You'd probably break it."

Before he could stop her, she touched it very gently with the tip of her smallest claw, and with a bright light, the screen came to life.

Pete gasped loudly, raising his hand to his face. "Oh wow! What did you do?"

Nat and Will shouted out in surprise.

Do you still doubt my magical powers? Quickly, come get a loose scale from the bottom of my other claw.

Pete tentatively reached out a hand to ease a scale from her paw.

Now gently press it onto a space at the edge of one of the keys.

Nat and Will watched openmouthed as the tiny, luminous, blue scale slowly sank into the keyboard.

Zara peered over Pete's shoulder "UN-BEE-LIEVE-ABLE! What just happened Pete?"

The kids were struck dumb as they gazed first at Jessynta, then at the tablet.

What are you waiting for? It is working. Show me what you do next. Jessynta tapped a paw up and down impatiently.

Will grinned from ear to ear. "I guess we get her to activate the other one I brought with me. I want to see why she wanted us to bring more than one!"

CHAPTER 17

THE AVALANYAN CHILDREN LOOKED on in puzzled amazement, listening and watching.

Brecky finally turned to Ven and shrugged her shoulders. "They really do have some strange ways. Did you ever see anything like those weird things they call tablets?"

Izzy sniffed loudly. "It's no use trying to understand anything when it's something to do with their world. I'll never understand them, however long I spend with them."

Lanya giggled. "At least life is never dull anymore, and it's a lot of fun wondering what they're going to do next."

Edwith and Rayvinith had long ago lost interest, and Crystalya nuzzled up closer to Ven, who was gently caressing her head.

When both tablets were working, Pete peered closer. "These are too low if they're on the ground. Put yours on that flat stone over there away from me, and I'll put mine on this one. Now open yours and press the link for me."

Nat complied.

"I see you on my screen, Nat, but move a little further away. We're still too close to each other. Can you see me?"

Nat moved to a different stone and tried again. "Wow! That's incredible. All without satellites!"

Edwith hopped closer to the screen to look and leaned over it.

Nat made a disgusted face. "Oh, yuck. Move away, Edwith. You're slobbering all over it."

Pete exclaimed, "I've got a close-up view of his snout now. "Come over here, Jessynta, and I'll show you how we do this video calling. Nat, turn the contact off, and we'll start over to show her how it's done."

She leaned over Pete's shoulder as he pressed the key for Nat. "When I press this key, Nat appears on my screen."

Yes, and I see Edwith behind him. Nathaniel, can you see me behind Peter?"

"I can, though of course only your head as you are rather big."

Hmm, I shall have to think about this. She tilted her head and looked down at the ground.

If you left this tablet with me, is there something I could touch to call you?

Will joined the pair to look. "I have an idea. Pete, you know how your fingerprint turns the screen on when you touch the home key? Show that key to Jessynta and how you press it with your thumb. Could you somehow get a print of Jessynta's claw and do something with it? Your print is programmed into the tablet."

Jessynta tapped her paw on the ground several times and turned her head from side to side. *I have it now, Peter. Touch my claw with your finger, and I will impress it into my mind.*

Pete shrugged his shoulders and put his finger on her claw.

Now turn this device off and move away. Nathaniel, turn off yours as well. We are starting over. When you are ready, reopen it.

They did as she said.

There was a loud shout from Nat. "Hooray! My tablet's working, and there's the new icon. Looks like a couple of waves. It's flashing. What do I do now?"

Do what you usually do and press it.

Nat yelled in delight. "I see you, Jessynta. You're on my screen. Amazing!"

Why do you doubt my magic?

Nat looked puzzled, shaking his head from side to side. "I can see you over there with Pete, and I also see you here on my screen, but I hear you in my mind. I don't understand any of this."

Will looked at Pete and Nat. "You know, I don't think we should worry about understanding it. Maybe it's because Jessynta is here, and you're hearing her in your mind as you normally do. It's not coming from your screen. Let's just accept that it's magic and go along with it. Pete, why don't you leave your tablet with Jessynta again? We'll take Nat's back home with us. It has Jessynta's icon, and it worked here, so it just might work at home."

Remember, there is a remote possibility my magic will not work in your world, because there is no magic there. However, mine is very powerful. As I will not be able to carry the tablet, perhaps Brecchettya could take it to my cave and open it for me when I need to use it.

Pete nodded in agreement. "Nat and I can share the other one." He handed it to Brecky who looked absolutely bewildered and was shaking her head in disbelief. "Look here. You don't have to do anything with it, or understand it, just don't drop it."

Brecky took it carefully from him.

Brechettya, later tonight when the boys are home, I shall test this new connection. You will have to pick the device up and stand it on one of these rocks here. You must open it for me. I will touch that home key with my claw. I am almost certain my embedded scale will cause it to call you, Peter. We can have that video chat you use. She fluttered her wings and preened herself.

Crystalya whimpered, and Zara rushed to pet her. "Oh, I'm so sorry. I have been ignoring you for so long."

Ven has been taking care of me. It is good to have two bond mates. She touched them with her wings. *Now stop playing with those things. Come and see the cave I have chosen. I want it to be the prettiest cave in the whole of Avalanya.* She fluttered her curling, purple eyelashes over her silver eyes. *Perhaps you can help me now. Jessynta gave me some of her light globes.*

Crystalya led the way, and they had a merry time decorating, using items taken from the other caves.

"As soon as we get back to our home in London, Mum will look for more goodies for you all," said Will. "There are many more shops there than where we are staying now."

"And I expect I can persuade my mother to look for some pieces too." Zara looked at Crystalya with pride when she raised her wings, fluttering them coyly. "Crystalya, we all know how lovely you are, so maybe you don't need to keep reminding us."

Jessynta tapped Crystalya's wing. *Zara has a point. You must not get too conceited. In my experience, humans do not care too much for boasting. You must let the praises come from them.*

Zara, will your mother bring goodies for us too? asked Edwith, touching Zara with a paw.

Zara patted Edwith's head. "Of course she will."

"The other day we were talking about power sources here in Avalanya," said Pete to Brecky. "You told us you live over underground heat sources and your father tapped into them to heat your water."

"We also have watermills with which we grind corn, and we have windmills. Before he left, our father was experimenting with making something to store the power from water. He dammed up a river and was trying to use it to make some kind of engine," said Izzy.

"That sounds like it might be something we know in our world as hydro-electric power," said Pete. "Maybe he was working on a battery. When we find your father, we might be able to help build one. I'll look for some pictures of ours to show him."

Ven joined in. "We should all try to find Uncle Brin. My father has a boat."

You children have the right idea, but it has to wait. It is part of my plan. We dragons must grow quite a bit more before we can undertake such a journey, and there is much more to be learned about our abilities.

"I think we have been here long enough today. Our father is coming to our vacation home tonight, so the next time we see you, we might have persuaded him to join us. That will be interesting. Wonder what he'll make of your use of the tablet," said Pete.

~~~~~

Their father stepped out of the car, and the boys rushed to him for a hug. "Hallo! I'm so glad to be through with work. Hope you haven't been too bored down here with no playmates. Nothing to do except laze around in the sun. Maybe now we can all spend some time together."

He looked closely at their faces. "What have you been up to? I know something's up, because Mum was unusually quiet on the way home. Out with it. What on earth is going on?"

"So much has happened, I don't know where to begin. Let's go inside," said Pete.

"Begin at the beginning. That's the usual thing." Dad laughed loudly at his own joke.

"I think it all began on the way down here. Mum might have told you I was a little distracted. That was because I was being called by a dragon in another universe."

"Oh, a new fantasy game for me to learn? You do come up with them!" said Dad. "I've missed playing games with you. So, what have you planned for me?"

Pete looked very solemnly at his dad. "No, this is no fantasy. Some people—even scientists—have brought up the subject of other universes from time to time. We now know that at least one exists, because we've all been there."
~~~~~

Dad made a face.

Will jumped in. "No really! There's no need to look like that!"

Pete began to tell him of their adventures, with a great many interruptions from his brothers.

Dad looked helplessly at Rachel. "Don't tell me you're in on this too?"

She touched his arm and smiled brightly. "I am indeed. I went with them the other day."

He frowned. "Right. Let's begin again: you went to this world or land or Avalanya or whatever it's called. You met some people, and you—what did you call it?—bonded with dragons. You're asking me to believe all this. And you want me to actually go with you tomorrow to meet them? All right then. Write down the rules so I can read them before I go to bed. I'll play with you tomorrow. I'm too tired tonight."

He stood and stretched. "It's nice and warm outside. I think I'll take a cold beer out there and enjoy the evening." Ignoring their pleading looks, he went to the kitchen, followed by Mum.

"Humph! That went well!" exclaimed Pete sarcastically. "Hopefully Mum will persuade him to believe us."

They sat still, listening to their parents talking outside, but it sounded as though their mother was getting upset and shouting at their father.

Finally, after what seemed like ages, he came back indoors, sat down, leaned back in the chair, tapped his hand impatiently on his knee, and prepared to listen. Pete had just begun the tale again when their mother called them into the kitchen to eat.

Their father sounded a little irritated. "Give it a rest while I eat, please, boys. We can carry on after dessert and a coffee."

Grim faced, they ate in forced silence.

Meal eaten and dishes cleared, the family settled down in the main room.

"All right, let's hear it all once again." After another

repetition of the tale, their father shrugged in resignation.

"Okay. I give in. I'll give you the benefit of the doubt. You have quite a story there, so I'm prepared to set off with you tomorrow. Did you also say these creatures can use your tablets?"

"Yes, that's right, although we can't understand how they do it. So, you will come with us in the morning then?"

"I still think it's a huge hoax, and I'm to be the victim of the biggest practical joke you have ever tried to play on me in your life. It will turn out to be just another dungeons and dragons game, like I said. Still, it will be something different. I need a bit of fun."

"You won't regret this. We promise."

Then leaving the room to their parents, they went into the back garden.

"Why don't we try to see if we can use our tablet to call Jessynta?" Carrying Nat's tablet, Pete set it up on a chair.

Nat pressed Jessynta's wave icon and waited eagerly.

Nat looked downcast. "It's not going to work."

Will touched his arm. "Patience. Remember Jessynta has to get Brecky to set it up for her. Look the icon is flashing."

"Yea! It's happening." Nat grinned in delight when Jessynta's face appeared on the screen.

Have you talked with your parents? Are they coming? asked Jessynta.

"Yes. It's all arranged for tomorrow in our world," said Pete. "Your voice is so much clearer. What did you do?"

I think it is because of the special bonding I did with you the last time we met. Can you see a mark on your body yet?

They looked and saw faint symbols at the top of their arms. They resembled bright tattoos about an inch long. Pete's looked like a blue water drop with a wave inside it.

Pete exclaimed. "Wow, it's like her icon on the tablet."

Will's tattoo resembled a reddish orange flame. Nat's was

three rainbow-colored clouds like mini whirlwinds.

"They're pretty, and they make sense considering what types of dragons we're bonded to," said Will.

"You said nobody else will be able to see them," said Nat. "That's actually a pity, because it would be good to show them to Dad. We had no end of a time trying to convince him of your existence."

All will be revealed to him tomorrow, will it not? We shall give them such a welcome, said Jessynta. Zara and Crystalya have not managed the shell connect yet, but I shall work on it a little more as soon as I can. The tablet connection might have to wait a bit because I am not sure if Crystalya is mature enough to understand it. Edwith and Rayvinith are here with me. Can you see them? I told them to stand well behind me.

"Yes, we can see them. Tell them to try speaking," said Will.

You will not be able to hear them, because I have not yet put their scales into the devices. I will take care of that when you are here. Edwith wants you to know that he had a great time with Zara. Rayvinith helped Crystalya move rocks around her cave. He burnt a few holes in the walls, and she found a lot of pretty gems there. We are making plans for your father's visit. Aleto, Zarven's father, will be here to mind meld with him, so you can finally meet him. I like him and Suki, his wife. She really liked meeting Zara and Crystalya. They are both looking forward to meeting you boys tomorrow. I showed Aleto your tablet, and he was very impressed. He wants one, but I would not let him touch it.

"It's good to hear all that and to be able to see Edwith, but I'm sad I couldn't talk to him with this tablet. I hope you'll be able to fix it tomorrow. The shells do still have their uses," said Nat.

Pete touched him and looked across at Will. "Don't worry. If Jessynta says she can fix it, she will. I don't believe we will need the shells for much longer. It's going to be much easier now that we have been marked and can use the tablets. There's something else I can show you tomorrow, Jessynta. A tiny camera inside the tablet. That's what makes images, and it can be turned around so we can see what you see."

I need to close this up, because it is draining a lot more magic than I had thought. Goodbye for now. She disappeared from the screen.

"Wow!" exclaimed Nat. "That was too amazing for words. Tablets working from another universe. If I hadn't seen it with my own eyes, I'd never have believed it. Makes me wonder what else Jessynta is capable of."

The rest of the evening dragged on, even though they tried to pass the time telling their father more about the dragons' version of their history.

"You know, Dad, if the people in our world could only see and hear what that world went through with the inhabitants polluting their planet, fighting wars, and killing lots of animals and bird species, they might listen to reason and do something about our planet. Although the dragons tried to help their people, nobody would listen to them. They even forbade them to come anywhere near them," said Nat.

"The dragons were banished to a faraway part of their world, so they didn't really see everything the humans were doing. Even the dragon species declined, not sure why, but I think it might have something to do with pollution and whole lots of animal species dying out as their habitats deteriorated. At least that's what Jessynta thinks," said Will.

Pete waved his hand. "It's all part of the reason we were called, so we can help them recover, and we can convince our people to wake up before it's too late."

"Sorry to disillusion you," said Dad, "but even if what you're saying is true—and mind you, I don't believe it for a moment— we couldn't help their world if all their technology is destroyed. We have taken thousands and thousands of years to get where we are today, and they wouldn't be able to understand our science."

Pete shook his head. "I said something to Jessynta about that, but she said they have something we never had on our world—magic."

Nat practically bounced in his seat. "That's one of the things that caused their world to go bad. Some of their magicians took over and ruled the world with powerful bad magic."

Their father looked at them sideways. "So what's different now?"

Pete scratched his head thoughtfully. "I'm not quite sure. A few people came to their senses, and after lots of battles, they overcame the bad guys and banished them. I don't know where they went. Jessynta may know, but for some odd reason, she won't say."

CHAPTER 18

"DAD IS REALLY IN for a surprise today, isn't he? I can't wait to see his face." Will was eager to eat breakfast and leave. "Can't we hurry them up?"

"No, remember, we should give Zara a chance to get there. We could hang out a little while here. Maybe we can go for a walk," answered Pete.

"I don't think it's necessary for us to be there at the same time as Zara. It would give Dad a little more time to do the mind meld and get adjusted to the place before she comes."

"Why don't we get our things ready? Get your tablet, Nat. Then we can go through everything with Dad as soon as they're up."

Nat went to fetch it. "I've got an idea. Why don't we have a quick chat with Jessynta while we're waiting?"

"I don't think that's a good idea. She won't be expecting us anyway, and we know it works. Let's just wait."

"Okay. I can't help feeling impatient though." He ran his hand through his hair.

"I think I hear movement upstairs. I'm sure they'll be down soon. We could start getting breakfast ready for them." Will got out plates and cups and put the kettle on.

Their mother walked into the kitchen. "Morning boys. Oh you started breakfast for us. Thank you. I know you're eager to get going." As soon as they finished eating, they rushed their parents outside.

Dad clapped his hands. "Right. Let's get this show on the road! Boys, where do we go? Up the hillside to this cave of yours?"

Will led them up the hillside to the woods and the cave entrance.

"I don't see anything but brambles and ivy," said Dad.

"Lead on, Pete. You had better get in front or it might not open," said Nat.

As Pete approached, the fronds waved gently. He gestured to Dad to walk behind him, followed by Will, then Mum, with Nat bringing up the rear.

As Pete parted the fronds and walked down the slope inside, the whole cave was lit up with so many bright globe lights, it looked like Christmas. As well as lights, the stalactites and stalagmites were studded with sparkling gems of different colors. Dad came to a sudden stop, almost tripping up Will.

"Gracious me, boys, you have outdone yourselves this time. This is truly magnificent. How did you get this done? I can see why you wanted me to see it, but was it really necessary to spin me that tremendous fantasy about worlds and dragons?" He pointed to the entrance to the cave where the dragons were lined up. "Who painted those dragons? The scenery looks so real apart from the pale green sky. BBUT . . . HOW . . . DDDID . . . YOU . . . GGGGETT . . . THEMMM . . . MOVING?" he stammered, blinking his eyes at the sight.

"It's okay, Dad. We all felt like that when we first saw it, but before we can do anything, you will have to mind meld with an Avalanyan. They speak a different language here. Stay here while I arrange it." Pete moved toward the cave entrance.

Spotting Ven standing beside a man he hadn't seen before Pete approached them. "Hi, Ven, is this your father? Hallo, sir. I'm Pete." He held out his hand.

The stranger took it. "So you are one of our son's new friends from another world? I didn't believe it at first. Pleased to meet you at long last. About time too! I am Aleto, and these other boys must be your brothers. Ven told me I have to meld minds with your father. Is this him? Poor guy! He looks absolutely mesmerized. Hope you told him what to expect."

Pete's father grabbed Pete's arm. "What's going on? Who is he? What's he saying to you? Do you know him? You were talking to him using strange words."

Pete faced his father. "Look at me, Dad. These folk live here in Avalanya. You must mind meld with one of them or you won't understand a word. You only have to do it once. We all did it, including Mum."

Hearing that, his father frowned and looked across at Rachel, but Pete pulled him over to Aleto. "Dad, I'm sorry about all this confusion, but I did warn you. Just let Aleto touch your head, and he'll do the rest."

Rachel had been standing very close watching anxiously. "It's okay, Paul. Look at me and relax. It will all become clear any minute now. I went through this too. Give me your hands." She clasped both his hands and placed them on Aleto's temples.

Paul looked at her and then at the stranger in front of him, who placed his own hands on him. Paul tried to shrink back but—

Do not be alarmed by hearing my voice in your head. My name is Aleto.

Everyone watched in silence. Paul's eyes widen in disbelief as Aleto made the contact. Paul's eyes flickered as the meld was taking place, and he withdrew after the contact was made.

Rachel took his arm again, and he turned to her with a questioning look.

"What an experience! If I hadn't felt that tingling, I'd have thought I was dreaming." He looked anxiously around the circle, taking several deep breaths. "Phew! I really didn't believe a word of your story, boys. How does this work? Pete, can they all understand me now? But I don't sound any different. You'd better introduce me one at a time to everybody."

Pete beckoned to Aleto. "Before I do, I thank you, Aleto, for doing the meld with our father, Paul. Ven kept trying to get us to meet you but somehow it never happened. We had better make up for lost time now!"

"You are most welcome. You haven't met my wife, Suki, either, so come on. Let's get to know each other."

There followed a flurry of introductions as the Avalanyan humans came over to meet them. The dragons stood still, unusually patient with their huge heads turning from side to side as they watched the humans greeting each other.

Pete clapped his hands dramatically and, in the biggest voice he could summon, said, "Now for the most important members of our group, without whom none of this could have happened!"

Jessynta stepped forward. *Peter, please tell your father to touch my head.* She bowed her head low.

"Dad, she needs you to touch her head, so you'll be able to hear her. Dragons speak telepathically."

Still with a bewildered expression on his face, Paul did as he was instructed.

Pleased to greet you, Revered Master Paul. I am Jessynta. We all are so happy to meet you and congratulate you on your excellent boys. It was also lovely to meet your lady wife Rachel. Dragons revere our parents greatly. I was the one who called your son Peter to this world and took him for my bond mate. I also have Brecchettya for my other bond mate. She gestured to Brecky with her wing.

"Watch out! Here comes trouble! Our resident clown Edwith," said Nat.

The dragon hopped forward in a shower of sand as he presented a rather muddy paw very graciously. *Pleased to meet you, Mr. Paul. Sorry about the sand. I am bonded to your son Nathaniel and Izchettya from Avalanya.* He waved his wing at Izzy, beckoning her to come forward.

"Call me Izzy." She wiped his hand free of Edwith's sand and mud.

Lanya and Will introduced Rayvinith, who lowered his feathery head for Paul to touch, and Lanya shook Paul's hand.

Welcome, sir. Sorry if I smell a little smoky. I have been practicing breathing fire. Do not be alarmed. You will not get burnt. I have almost perfect control of it now.

Suddenly there was a loud shout, and Zara ran up to the group with Crystalya hopping behind her.

"Hi, Uncle Paul and Aunt Rachel. Bet you didn't expect to see me here, did you? Just look at my gorgeous friend Crystalya, the most beautiful dragon in the world. I wanted to have my parents here as well, but Jessynta said it would mix up the time stuff or something like that if too many of you were here at the same time. We have to fix up my portal for them first anyway." Stopping for breath she waved to Ven. "Hi, Ven! He's bond mate to Crystalya with me.

Paul looked dazed as Crystalya lowered her head to him. After he had patted her head, Rachel approached and placed a hand on the newest dragon's head as well. "I don't think we've met yet."

Pete noticed his father was looking a little unsteady. "Dad, you don't look too good. I think you had better sit down."

"Oh dear me," said Skyla apologetically. "I am so sorry. I should have realized how you would be feeling. You do look a bit wobbly. It will be the shock. Come and sit here on this pile of soft blankets. In fact, let's all sit down and give our latest earth visitor a chance to recover. It must be so overwhelming. It was easier for us, because we met the dragons one at a time. Have some of this fruit juice first. I'll spread out the food while you relax a little. Don't try to talk, just look around, and listen."

She offered everybody orange-colored fruit juice and laid out plates of food. When they were all settled down, Aleto produced bottles of ale. "Hope you drink ale, Paul. I brew it myself."

Suki, who had not said much before, approached Rachel and offered her a glass of sparkling white liquid. "You might prefer some wine I have from our very own grapevines. It's from a vintage a couple of seasons ago, and it was a very good year."

Paul recovered his voice and raised his glass to Aleto. "Cheers and thank you. This is great."

Rachel took a sip from her glass. "Mmmm, this is indeed delicious. One would have to travel a long way in our world to find a wine as good as this."

Paul laughed loudly. "I think this is far enough, don't you?" He poked her gently in the ribs with a smile. This seemed to break the tension, and everyone laughed.

Edwith slapped his tail up and down, sending clouds of sand into the air and causing everyone to cover their plates. *Can we eat now?*

"Be careful, Edwith, you'll get sand in our food." Nat tapped his wing playfully. He pointed to the loaves of bread. "Skyla bakes this every day, and she makes the cheese."

"Suki made the rolls and that creamy sauce you're all dipping them into," said Skyla. "The fruit comes from our orchard."

Zara picked up a piece of fruit which looked a little like a purple watermelon. "Ooh, this is really yummy. You should taste this, Crystalya." She took a slice over to her. Ven gave her yellow cheese, which she liked as well.

Paul, after tasting both the ale and the wine, smacked his lips. "I don't know what I like best: the wine, the ale, or all this food."

Everyone sat back, eating, exchanging tales, and discussing

the things their children had been up to over the last few days.

The dragons, too, were enjoying their food: fresh fish for Jessynta, meat for Edwith and Rayvinith, and lots of delicious fruit, salad greens, and nuts for Crystalya. Edwith, of course, ate some of everything and even drank the ale and wine. Indeed, he consumed a large bowl of the wine and burped loudly making everyone laugh.

Shcuse me, he said, his speech sounding slurred even in their minds.

You had better not drink any more of that, scolded Jessynta.

Shtop spoiling my fun. You may be the Queen, but you are not my mother.

Jessynya prodded him with the end of her wing. *I will excuse you this time, because you were so patient earlier and managed to wait while all the humans greeted each other, but do not make a habit of talking back to me.*

"Don't take any notice of Edwith's comments," said Nat to his father. "He carries on like that all the time."

The adults laughed, even Paul, who was starting to enjoy himself, judging from the expression on his face.

Rayvinith ate a lot of food and was horrified when he burped, and with it, he expelled a large gout of flame. It almost burnt Edwith, who turned to him with a raised paw, ready to retaliate.

Nat hastily intervened. "Edwith, it's a good job you aren't a fire dragon, or you could catch our whole picnic on fire!" He tapped Edwith's paw playfully.

Will patted Rayvinith. "When you can really control your flame, we can have a great barbecue."

Jessynta was ready to change the subject. *I think now we can discuss your tablets. Put one tablet on this rock for me please, Peter. Nathaniel, put the other one on that rock over there.* She waved her wing over to a rock a bit farther away. *Edwith and Rayvinith, please come close to me and give me two each of your smallest scales. Down near your claws will do. I will touch you first so that it will not hurt at all.*

Watching the two dragons easing the scales off their paws, Paul opened his eyes wide. He grabbed Pete's arm. "What is she doing?"

Pete hurriedly explained to his father that Jessynta was able to work their tablets with magic and how she had been able to do video chats the day before. "I didn't tell you before we got here, because it was too much for you to believe all at once. Sorry."

"You're right, I can't take all this in. I do hope there isn't much more. Just sitting here in a land with a green sky and four enormous mythical creatures is almost too much. But this is truly amazing." He moved closer.

Peter, press one of each dragon's scales on your tablet. Nathaniel, do the same with the other one.

They did as she asked and watched the scales melt into the tablets. Then two new icons appeared on each tablet.

Will leaned forward to look. "Oh, there's a flame like the tattoo mark on my arm. Nat, there's your whirl-windy one that must be for Edwith."

Pete said, "Jessynta, I need to show you how to turn the built-in camera around so we can see what's in front of you. But this is something that needs to be done by human hands. Brecky, can you come here?"

Pete guided her hand to the screen. Look at this screen. Do you see a little image with a circle in it?"

She raised her eyebrows but slowly nodded.

"That is the thing which produces the images you see on the screen, but now it only shows the person who is in front of it. It's called a camera." Pete pronounced the word slowly. "All you must do is tap this button gently, and it will turn the camera around." He pointed to another button on the screen.

"Oh, the picture on the front has changed. Come over here,

Izzy. You can see Edwith and Rayvinith over there with Lanya," said Brecky in surprise.

Edwith had been watching all this with interest. *Ooh I want to see what I look like.* He rushed over. *But I do not see me, just Rayvinith and Lanya.*

Pete grinned at him and pointed to where Rayvinith was still standing. "You were there, but you left the scene. If you want to see yourself, I must press another key to take a still image. Go back there and I'll do it."

When Edwith saw himself on the screen, his mouth dropped open. *Fun! Do it again while I am over there. Now point it at me again. Yippee! A new game.* He proceeded to play around in front of the tablet. *Come on, Rayvinith, breathe out some fire. Hey, not at me! Peter, get a picture of me doing this.*

Edwith clowned around in great glee, posing in different positions, even attempting to stand on his front claws only. Of course, being Edwith, he ended up on his snout!

Stop! Stop! Enough of that. This is serious, said Jessynta.

Edwith bowed his head to her in apology, but everyone found it difficult not to laugh at him.

Zara pouted with indignation, crossing her arms in front of her. "It isn't fair of you, Jessynta. What about me and Crystalya?"

I am so sorry, Zara. She is so new to all this. I cannot try it too soon. However, I will see tomorrow. Perhaps you can get here earlier and bring your tablet. I can fix yours up. Also, if Mother Skyla's workmen have finished working on your portal, your parents can come with you.

Zara shrieked in delight. "Ooh, that's great, thank you! Thank you! That will be super, won't it, Crystalya?" She threw her arms excitedly around her dragon's neck.

Aleto had a broad grin. "I don't know what amazes me most about all this. The stuff you earth people have or all this magic. All I came to do was a simple mind meld. I wish I had one of those tablet things." He scratched his chin.

"Can we use this tablet as normal when we get home? Will it still work as it used to? What happens if somebody else gets ahold of it and tries to use it?" asked Nat.

The connection will not work for anyone but you three, as you alone are linked to us. The new—what did you call them?—icons will not be visible to anyone else.

Paul had been sitting watching all this in fascination. "This I have to see." He shook his head from side to side and sighed heavily. "It just isn't feasible, and yet you did it without any connection to any satellites. Let me try it." He moved to touch the tablet closest to him. "I don't see any new icons. What happened to them?"

It will only work for your boys. It is only tuned to them.

"Something like that could be really useful in our world. People continually try to break into our private systems. What a pity we don't have any of your magic," said Paul.

Some people in the past used it for bad purposes. In the old days, I understand that a few of our creatures did manage to appear briefly in your world, although they were unable to stay there.

Pete nodded. "That might be how some of our myths came into being."

Possibly, but after Avalanyans got rid of our bad magicians, they closed all portals and banished us. Our memories do not tell us what happened after that. Our world got hotter, and our climate changed. There were many earthshakes and floods, and the area we inhabited got smaller and smaller. This is why the dragons began to lay eggs for the future.

"Well, you really have given us so much to think about. What's going to happen to our world if we continue on as we are doing at present?" said Paul with a large frown.

Will had been listening intently to Jessynta with a puzzled expression. "So where did the Avalayans send the bad guys?"

Jessynta lowered her head and looked at the ground. *Oh,*

dear, I hoped you would not ask me that. I am sorry to tell you that they sent them to your world. That is why they closed all the portals, so magicians could not return. She closed her eyes and sank to the ground.

Paul shook his head from side to side in silent denial.

Aleto clasped Suki's hand as they looked at each other in surprise.

Paul finally found his voice. "What a terrible thing to do. How could they have done that?" He looked at Jessynta and the rest of the Avalanyans with unspoken questions in his eyes, still shaking his head.

Jessynta raised her head and looked Paul in the eye. *I can see you are angry, and I agree with you. Please forgive this world. It was millions of years ago, and our world suffered a great deal since then. It was nothing to do with the dragons. We were powerless to prevent it. The Avalanyans did not think too much harm could be done by the bad guys as there was no magic on your world. It does not surprise me that you feel this way. I can only ask you all to put it behind you. We have to concentrate on helping each other's world as best we can.*

Paul and Rachel looked at each other doubtfully. Then Paul closed his eyes for a few minutes, deep in thought.

Everyone held their breath.

Squaring his shoulders and taking a deep breath, Paul opened his eyes. "You're right. We should help each other, and there is a great deal to do."

CHAPTER 19

AS THEY WALKED DOWN the hillside to the cottage, Paul and Rachel couldn't stop talking about the whole adventure.

"It all seems so much like a dream. I'm feeling rather strange having gone through all that," said Paul. "Although I do have to admit to being very tired."

Once indoors, they sat down to have a drink and discuss the day's events.

"I'm very impressed with those creatures, especially that dragon Jessynta," remarked Paul. "I wonder if there's anything we could do to help the Avalanyans redevelop some kind of technology of their own. Without factories, there's not much they'll be able to accomplish."

"Still, they do seem to have things on their side which we don't, not least, their ability to use magic," said their mother.

Their father narrowed his eyes. "I wasn't very pleased to hear about the original inhabitants sending their criminals to our world. That was a bit of a dirty trick in my opinion."

Will looked thoughtful and rested his chin on his hand. "Do you think those bad guys might have been behind some of the terrible things which happened in our world?"

Dad quickly turned to look at him. "I hardly think so. It sounds as though it was long ago, before there was even much civilization around. They could well have had an impact on early tribal wars though. Anyway, we can't worry about it now. It was in the ancient past. We have more pressing concerns about our own future."

After they had eaten dinner, their parents decided to relax and have an early night. The boys went outside to see if the new icons would let them hear the other dragons.

"Okay, let's have a go," said Pete when they had reached the chairs at the top of the hill.

After several anxious minutes, Jessynta's face appeared on the screen. *Hello. Is this good?*

"Yes. Where are Edwith and Rayvinith? Can we try talking to them as well?" asked Will.

They are here. I will get Edwith to sit beside me. Touch his icon so you can hear him.

Large, slimy nostrils appeared on the screen. "Ooh, yuck! That's not a pretty sight. You're way too close. Back off," said Nat.

A loud sound came from the tablet. *Ouch! No need to shove me. I'll move.*

The boys burst out laughing. "Oh, no! Edwith the clown must have struck again," said Nat. "No, come closer slowly. You're too far now."

"Jessynta, ask Brecky to turn the camera, then we can see them both at once. You're too big to share the screen. There you are. Hi, Edwith. Hi, Rayvinith. I can see all three of you at once. It all works splendidly, Jessynta," said Pete. "Your magic seems to be working well with our devices. Do you think you can use them to move our portal though?"

Yes, now that I have seen all the things your devices are capable of, I have a good idea of what I can do. It will involve them and the shells. You said you can make permanent images on them? And make changes to them?

"Yes, we can. No problem. We call them photos, and we can alter them."

What I have in mind should be fairly simple. I will explain it to you when you come to Avalanya again. You said you know how to get the exact position of your home, did you not?

"Oh, yes," answered Pete. "Latitude and longitude are invisible lines that scientists mapped around our earth. Using them, our satellites can tell our position exactly. But we had better do this fairly soon as we have little time left now."

Next time we meet, we shall use your device to take images of your portal here. It is actually better to leave it until close to your departure, because once we alter things, we will not be able to use this one for many more days. It is tuned to you, but I do not want to leave an open portal. When you activate your new one, I will close this one permanently. Now we must go, as this tends to drain my magic. Come along, Edwith and Rayvinith, say goodbye.

The last image the boys saw was that of Edwith chasing Rayvinith who was shooting flames along the beach.

"Wonder what Rayvinith did to annoy Edwith." Nat tried to stifle his laughter.

"I wonder if Zara is back home yet. Let's try a video chat with her and tell her about this latest development with the tablets." Will pressed video chat.

"Hi, you all. That was an exciting day, wasn't it? Mum still can't believe me when I talk to her about it. I told her Jessynta said they could come to visit. Skyla's men have finished making my portal easier for them, so we're ready. Suki said she can do the meld with Mum. She's one of the few who can meld with multiple people."

"Don't forget to take a tablet with you," said Pete.

"I've got a spare ready. Can your parents explain the mind meld to my parents first? I don't think they completely understood me."

"Sure thing," Will said.

"It's getting a bit dark here, so I'll have to go indoors. See you in Avalanya tomorrow." Zara signed off.

Later that night before bed, the boys talked a bit more about the day and wondered about moving the portal to their home.

"I can't help worrying about it though, and whether it will work," said Nat.

"I worry too, but I think Jessynta seems to be more on top of things now. She certainly got the tablets working. Have you considered how unusual it is that our mother doesn't seem to be too bothered about us going off on our adventures? I'm wondering if Jessynta, with her magic and thought transference, is somehow influencing our parents to relax." Pete sat on the bed.

"That had occurred to me too," answered Nat. "It really isn't normal for her to be so relaxed. She certainly wasn't before she met Jessynta."

Will leaned in the doorway. "With all the magic stuff Jessynta can do, it wouldn't be at all surprising if she could influence them, and with that, I include Dad. After the initial shock, he really came round to it all, didn't he?"

"It could help a lot if she can reassure them if everything gets more complicated," said Pete.

"What do you mean? More complicated?" asked Nat

Pete tapped his forehead. "I don't know, but I'm sure Jessynta has a lot more things in her mind she hasn't told us about yet."

~~~~~

"Morning, Dad. Were you able to explain anything to Uncle Mark last night? Are they going with Zara today?" Pete asked.

"Yes, I spoke with him, but until he actually experiences it, I can't explain it easily. Let me know how he and Anita get on. I'm sure there will be another feast laid on, especially if Edwith has anything to do with it."

Nat was fidgeting around, obviously eager to leave. "Come on, you two, let's go now."
~~~~~

The moment they arrived in Avalanya, Edwith rushed up to them. *Hurry up or you will miss the feast. Mother Skyla is laying it out now.*

Zara waved them over excitedly. "There you are! Come and say hallo to Mum and Dad. Crystalya has fallen completely in love with my mother. Look at them both."

Aunt Anita sat on the sand, petting the dragon who sounded like she was purring. "Zara told me she was beautiful, but I thought she was exaggerating. How are you boys? I gather you started all this."

They hugged their aunt and said hallo to Uncle Mark. "It's great to see you two and quite a unique way to meet. I didn't actually start all this; it was Jessynta." Pete went over to the dragon and stroked her muzzle. "More grownups to join our group now. This is fun. I see Edwith is tucking in."

Izzy quickly looked at Edwith and took the carafe of wine out of his way. "Behave, Edwith. You don't want to make Jessynta mad at you. Drink this lovely fruit juice. Nat, taste this juice Aunt Suki brought."

Anita patted the sand next to her. "Come and sit by me. Suki and I have discovered we have something in common. We both play a musical instrument. Hers is called a Lyricon, and it sounds just like my cello. The next time we come, she's going to play it for me. I'll try to bring mine. That really will be an out-of-the-world duet, won't it?" She hugged herself at the thought.

"I've been talking about our hydro-electric power with Aleto, and even though he found it difficult to understand, he's going to think hard about making a battery. He seems to have an unusual feel for metal and is amazingly talented at tool making," said Mark. "Young Ven seems keen, and he's talented as well. I'm going to look for pictures of early discoveries of ours to give them some ideas."

Nat was eager to learn if Jessynta had managed to work

with Zara's tablet. "What does your icon look like, Zara? Show me. Oh, that figures. Crystalya is an earth dragon, so that's leaves, and maybe that purple round thing is an amethyst. That reminds me, did Crystalya put those gems on the stalactites in our entryway?"

"Yes. She said Rayvinith burnt holes in the walls, and she found the gems there."

Mark was looking over their shoulders at the tablet. "What are you talking about? It looks the same to me."

"Jessynta says only the people who are bond mated to dragons can see them," said Nat.

Mark opened his eyes wide in surprise. "Great security. I bet your father approves of that."

"Jessynta seems very confident these days, and all the dragons appear to be maturing much more rapidly than I would have imagined possible," said Nat. "Even our Edwith is beginning to act a little more sensibly."

"Jessynta's making them practice flying every day. They are so much bigger, and their wing struts are strengthening." Brecky stroked Jessynta's side.

The day passed all too quickly, and Pete was surprised to see it was time to leave. Standing up, he hugged his aunt. "Don't you wish it was as easy as this to meet up instead of flying on a plane for seven hours? I wish our parents could be here at the same time. What a party we could have." He tilted his head to one side, looking wistful.

Nat nodded. "Jessynta's magic skills are so amazing that it wouldn't surprise me if one of these days she'll work out how to get over the limitations she talked about."

<div align="center">~~~~~</div>

The next morning Nat crunched his breakfast cereal noisily. "Yesterday was quite a day, wasn't it? My guess is that it won't be too long before we can actually ride on our dragons." Scraping his bowl, he beamed.

"That's one thing I'm not looking forward to." Will shuddered.

"Our parents will really freak out when they hear we may be flying soon," said Nat. "I'm glad nobody mentioned that possibility to Uncle Mark and Aunt Anita. I'd prefer to break the news to our parents first."

"I wonder how Lanya is getting on with the saddles. Now of course she has to make one for Crystalya too."

"I'm not quite as excited as you are at the prospect, and I know Will isn—" Pete suddenly froze.

"What's up? Is something wrong?" Nat looked at him anxiously.

"No, it's just that I'm hearing Jessynta's voice in my head. That's unusual." He scratched his arm.

Nat looked at Will. "I don't hear anything, do you?"

Will shook his head.

"I'll get my tablet." Nat fetched it from his room and gave it to Pete who eagerly pressed Jessynta's icon.

"Hi, Jessynta, did you want to talk to me?"

Yes, I do. I have worked out exactly how to do your portal move, and I am ready now. Can you bring your father? You said he knows a lot about how your devices work, and he might be needed.

"He's asleep. I'll have to wake him. I'm sure our parents will be happy to meet you again. They've talked about it non-stop since their last visit, but I hope they won't get too tired. We'll have to watch them."

When you are ready, set your tablet up by the door of the portal and summon me.

"What do you mean summon you?"

Just think of me in your mind and press the icon. See you in a short while with your parents. Bring the shells.

Rachel entered the kitchen. "Morning, Mum," Pete said. "Jessynta wants to sort out the portal today. Can you wake

Dad? When you have eaten your breakfast, we need to get ready to go."

Dad came into the kitchen. "Morning, everyone. Go? Where?"

"Jessynta wants to do the portal move and needs you."

"Sure thing. It'll be fun to meet those fantastic creatures again. Just give me time to drink a cup of tea and get some toast."

"Let's take some treats with us. Perhaps some of our fruits, crackers, nuts, and drinks." Their mum bustled around collecting items.

"I think I have a couple of bottles of nice wine to take with us," added their dad.

Soon the excited group made their way up the hillside, laden with a bag of goodies and the tablet. As they approached the cave entrance, Pete called Jessynta in his mind. He found a suitable rock to set up the tablet. "We're here. Are you ready?" He jumped when he saw Jessynta in front of them inside the rock doorway.

"Oh!" he exclaimed, raising his hands to his face. "I never expected to see you here in our world." He leaned forward to touch her, and his hand went right through her body. "Oh my days! You're not really here at all. What magic is this?"

Will clapped excitedly. "I know! She's a hologram like you see in movies."

I know you are surprised. I cannot actually visit your world, so I thought of this. I discovered a new piece of magic, but it really is draining on me physically. We must be quick. This has to be done outside the portal. Revered Master Paul, will you take an image with the tablet?

"You mean take a photo?"

Yes, set it up to take a photo of the portal entrance, but do not do it until I tell you. Boys, do you have shell pieces with you?

They held up their pieces of shell.

Place one at the top of the door to the portal where the rock opening is, and the other two on either side. Try to make them line up with the opposite side. Do not worry about being too accurate with the height of the shell pieces, just one each side will do, at approximately Peter's height or even a little higher if you can.

"How can we stick them up there? We don't have glue," said Will.

They are magic shells.

The boys exchanged knowing looks.

Boys, make a small tight circle in front of the portal with each of you holding a piece of shell. Make sure you are touching each other and stand as close together as you can. Master Paul, will you please take a photo of the three of them and the rock opening all together? Boys, stand as still as you can. Do not move or be surprised at what happens next.

After Paul had taken the picture, Jessynta's body began lengthening as she slowly moved around them. It was hard not to move as the portal began to glow and shimmer. A bright blue light encircled them.

Now take another image, Master Paul.

The resulting flash blinded them for a moment, but nobody was hurt. Shivering in surprise, they gasped. When their eyes had adjusted from the blinding flash, Jessynta's tail was disappearing into the portal.

They gazed at each other as if mesmerized.

"Well, I never!" Paul looked at the tablet. "That was surprising, but I got a photo. Come and look!"

Recovering from the shock, they rushed to look. He had indeed captured a photo, although Jessynta appeared merely as a faint outline. Puzzled, they studied it until Will made a suggestion. "Perhaps it was because she was only a hologram. Look she's normal size again, but she's still a hologram."

Jessynta shimmered just inside the entrance. *Now, you*

must add your latitude and longitude to this photo.

"Not necessary. The camera adds that automatically when we take a picture. Still, I'll make a note of it just in case." Paul tapped his forehead.

When you return to your real home, do not forget to give me its coordinates. Then you boys are to look for a suitable place to site the new portal. As soon as you have decided, stick your pieces of shell in approximately the same positions around the edges as you have done here, making sure that the top is the height of a real door. Of course you should find a very private situation where no strangers are likely to see it. Even though it will not actually be visible to anyone other than you, it is better to be safe.

Will said, "What about the summer house at the end of our garden? Nobody but us goes behind it, and there's a fence screening us from the neighbors plus a lot of shrubs and tall trees. From the outside, it just looks like a normal summer house."

"Great idea, Will." Nat gave him a thumbs up. "Presumably it won't really make a hole in the wall. It'll be like a magic doorway which will only open for us, rather like the wardrobe in Narnia."

As I understand, you can take an image of your proposed doorway when you get there and meld the two images together, making it look as though the two images are one. When you have done it, call me, and I shall do the rest.

"What happens if the new portal will not activate?" asked Nat, doubtful as always.

Then I shall just find another way. Now that we have finished the business part of today, come through and join us.

They gathered up their belongings and entered the portal.

"Wow," exclaimed Will when they emerged on the other side of the cave. "I do believe you've grown again, Rayvinith. I'd better keep well out of your way when you breathe fire or I might get scorched."

I would never hurt any of you.

Look how big I am too, said Edwith as he pushed forward eagerly to receive a pat from Nat.

We do not really know how long it will take us to grow to our full size, said Jessynta. *We usually grow in our sleep. Although there are some amongst us who seem to grow continually.* She turned her head to gaze at Edwith.

"How did you make yourself so much longer when you appeared in hologram form?" asked Pete.

Some of us can change shape in different ways. You will see later when we are a little older. We have many more skills to master.

"There is a legendary creature in our world called the Loch Ness monster," said Will. "It strikes me that it could have been a dragon like you, as it is snakelike and reputedly had a long neck."

It possibly could have been, but that is not in my mother's memory. There used to be many more dragons other than my family. Some dragons do have the ability to morph into other creatures or things. It remains to be seen if the others can, although I think it is only a female ability.

Pete noticed Will staring into the middle distance. "Will, you're miles away. Are you still thinking about the Loch Ness monster?"

Will shook his head. "No, I've just had another of my ideas. Do you remember watching people hang gliding off cliffs? They have perfect cliffs around here. The dragons could start at the top of one, spread their wings, and glide down. There are air pockets they could catch and learn to glide left or right. I've watched people. They have sails like wings made of fabric which are attached to a harness. I've never done it, of course, but I think they move to left or right by pulling on straps attached to them."

Nat clapped his hands in excitement. "Clever old you. Of

course! Jessynta, if you dragons glided, it would strengthen your wings and teach you how to control your movements."

Jessynta raised her head. *My mother talked about air movements. She called them thermals. Perfect, and it would really help with the exercises I have been giving them. Edwith can already fly quite a bit, even without a jump from the top of a hill. He has been really surprising and working so hard. This could be fun. Rayvinith could try too. I could use some help catching thermals as well.* She reached out with a paw to gently touch Will, who beamed with pride.

Ooh, can you get us some of those fabric sails? asked Edwith, flapping his tail up and down.

Nat burst into laughter. "You silly goose, you don't need fabric sails. You have wings of your own." He stroked Edwith's closest wing.

Edwith jumped to his paws. *Me first. Follow me up to the top of the cliff. Come along, Rayvinith.*

Nat quickly said, "Just the lowest one on this side first. Then with practice, you can progress to the higher ones."

There soon followed a hectic exhibition of climbing and gliding as the two competed with each other.

Rachel was highly amused. "You are pretty fantastic. Rayvinith is particularly spectacular. I think his feathers help. He's almost like a bird anyway."

Zara ran up in time to see a fantastic glide up and down in the air by Rayvinith. Crystalya and Ven followed close behind Zara. "What are you doing? Looks like fun. Is it a new game? Are we too late to join in? Hurry up, Aleto and Suki, come and watch this." She beckoned Ven's parents forward. They watched as Edwith and Rayvinith showed off their new gliding skills.

"What about Crystalya?" asked Ven.

I think she needs to wait a while longer. Her wing struts need to be stronger. Jessynta stretched her wing protectively over the little dragon. *They are growing very fast though. You are surprising even me.*

Zara stroked Crystalya. "There you are, my pet. She says it won't be long before you can join the others." She turned to greet Paul and Rachel. "Great to see you again, Uncle Paul and Aunt Rachel. Mum and Dad had such a wonderful time visiting here. Mum loved all the dragons but especially loved Crystalya. Look how big she is now." Zara stroked the dragon as she talked.

I think after we have eaten, we can discuss our plans for flying, said Jessynta.

"You have plans for us to fly soon? Pete stared at her.

Rachel grabbed hold of Paul's arm. "I'm not so sure about that."

They took a step toward Jessynta who sat and lowered her head to them.

Pete caught Nat's hand and whispered in his ear. "Look at her. She's talking privately to them. I told you she could influence them. Wonder what she's saying? Whatever it is, watch their faces. They don't look as worried now."

Jessynta raised her wings to get everyone's attention. *They will be quite safe. For one thing, I shall be in charge of it all, and I will put a magic spell on them to make sure they do not fall off. My mother passed on her memories of flying and how to take care that youngsters do not overdo things.*

That does sound exciting, but can we not eat first? said Edwith.

That relieved the tension. Everybody laughed. Skyla produced a large rug and laid out wooden plates, knives, and glasses. Rachel brought out their contributions and Paul his wine. These last items caused a lot of interest and questions from the Avalanyan folk. Crystalya was delighted to see the fruit and nuts which were nothing like any that she had seen.

Oh, no you do not! said Jessynta when she saw Edwith about to down a large amount of wine. *You can only have a little as it makes you dizzy.*

I am really thirsty though.

"That's no problem," said Skyla. "I didn't forget you. Look, I brought a large container of lemonade for you and the other dragons."

"We brought fizzy drinks from our world too." Nat brought out bottles of sodas. "Although if we continue to eat and drink like this every time we come here, we'll gain weight. I must be catching this hunger thing from Edwith."

"You may be right," said Izzy. "I swear I never used to eat so much or so often either."

I do not force you to eat. You can say no, and I could eat your share, said Edwith.

We are not all as greedy as you, friend Edwith. Rayvinith waved a wing at him.

CHAPTER 20

AFTER THE EXCITEMENT OF gliding, they all settled down to relax. Paul sat beside Aleto. "So you like to work with metal and make things. What else do you do?"

"We like to play ballgames like kick ball. What about you in your world?"

"We do a lot of that and other outdoor games, running and jumping, but we also play special games around a table indoors. We play imaginary games on our devices like fights with aliens and something called Dungeons and Dragons."

Aleto leaned forward, raising his eyebrows. "Dragons! But I thought you didn't have them in your world."

"For us, dragons are only characters in films, books, or games which artists have drawn. We have gadgets with which we can make them move and fight each other."

Aleto frowned. "I don't understand. Film? Gadgets to make them move? Like your tablets?"

Ven poked his father. "Don't even try. These earth people have all kinds of strange devices and gadgets."

"We also have board games. Large pieces of board with little toys and cards we move around it to gain points." Seeing Aleto was still puzzled, he said, "Best if I bring a game here one day and show you."

"Sounds interesting. We don't have anything like that. "

Rachel looked at Suki. "Anita told me you play a lyricon. I'd like to hear that some time. We love music in our world."

Edwith was tapping his paw. *Enough of all this chatter. We have things we can do too. I have a surprise for you all as well. I have been learning to fly, and I am getting quite good, am I not, Jessynta? How would you like to try a flight with me, Nathaniel?*

Rachel jumped to her feet in shock. "You want to take our son up in the air today? I didn't know it would be so soon. No way! Not today. I need more time to think about it, and Paul agrees with me. Don't you?" She grabbed his arm. "Jessynta, tell me this isn't going to be now?"

Jessynta sat between Rachel and Paul. She touched them gently with one of her paws.

Pete, his brothers, and Zara huddled together looking very anxious. "I can't hear what Jessynta's saying to them. Can you?" whispered Pete.

They shook their heads. Rachel held Paul's hand as Jessynta continued to watch them keenly. The children heard her this time.

You must not worry about this, Revered Mother Rachel and Master Paul. I shall be in contact all the time when they fly. Izchettya has already been up with Edwith. Tell them, Mother Skyla.

"It's true. I was scared out of my wits the first time I saw it, but he was so gentle, almost a changed dragon. Lanya has made extremely safe saddles, and Izzy was so well fastened in, she couldn't jump out, let alone fall. He didn't go higher than the roof of a house, and they flew over the edge of the sea. Fetch the saddles, Izzy."

Thus reassured, Rachel and Paul both agreed but still looked a bit grim faced.

"I want a close look at this saddle. It does look strange. I guess the boots on the end of the stirrups would stop feet slipping out. There are lots of straps and belts. Okay, you may try, Nat."

Nat grinned broadly at his mother. "Thanks, Mum. I'll be fine. Will Izzy and I ride together?"

No. That is for the future. It is much too soon for the dragons to fly with two of you, so at first, you are each going to take flight separately. Mother Rachel, relax.

Skyla said, "Please trust her. You can have the utmost confidence in Edwith. He has shown himself to be extremely conscientious and flies very gently and carefully."

Edwith sat tall and gently waved his wings. *You shall see, Madam Rachel.* He bowed his head slowly to her. *I am proud to be the first dragon chosen to make this flight with Nathaniel. As you will see, I will fly as low as I can and above the sea, not that there is the slightest danger of Nathaniel falling.* He shook his wings with pride.

Rachel watched anxiously while Nat was helped up. Izzy buckled a sturdy belt around his waist and attached it to the saddle. She fingered the extra-long girth straps fastened around Edwith's stomach. "These look very strong. Lanya, well done! It's a very well-made saddle. I just hope it's as strong as it looks." She shuddered slightly, and her forehead creased in anxiety.

Try to relax and hold onto the spike in front of the saddle. I will not let you fall but be ready for a slight jerk when I actually leave the ground. You might feel a little nauseous at first, said Edwith.

"You'll be fine," said Izzy. "I felt a little queasy, but it passed. Just in case, here's a little bag." She quietly handed him a small cloth bag. "Good luck and enjoy."

She stood back, and they all watched as Edwith bent his front limbs, pumped his enormous wings, and took a leap into the air.

"Wow! Yippee! Wonderful!" yelled Nat at the top of his voice. "Better than any ride I've ever been on." A broad grin spread across his face.

For the first few minutes, Paul watched, his brows furrowed in concentration. Rachel peeked through her hands. When they saw how smoothly and carefully Edwith soared through the air, they began to relax. However, both of them strained as hard as they could to keep the duo within sight as they made circuit after circuit of the air above the edge of the sea.

It feels so good to fly with you. It is as though I was designed for you. I am so happy; I could fly forever and ever.

Better not, Jessynta warned. *I am timing you, Edwith. You must not strain yourself too much yet. You may not think so, but you are still a young dragon. Be good now, or I shall forbid the rest of the outing for you and ground you for several weeks!*

All right, boss.

Do not be cheeky, young Edwith. However you must come down now. That is enough for one day.

Edwith circled around over the shallows and landed with only a few bumps. Rather shakily, Nat climbed down as soon as his buckles and straps were released. His legs almost gave way, but as his mother rushed forward, he steadied himself. He gave Edwith a huge pat and praised him profusely.

Everybody gathered around, praising him as well.

Jessynta said, *Well done, Edwith. I am very proud of you, and well done, Nathaniel.*

Lanya and Rayvinith had been watching this enviously, although Will was frowning and did not look at all excited.

Gulllanya and Rayvinith, it will be a while longer for you as you have not spent too long in the air and need more practice. Zara and Zarven, you and Crystalya too must wait as she is even younger.

Will could not help a sigh of relief, but Zara, Lanya, and Ven looked dejected. The two dragons lowered their heads.

The next to fly will be Peter and Brechettya who, although they have ridden on my back, it was only in the water, and they have yet to fly.

Honored parents of Nathaniel, when I am a lot older and stronger, it would be my greatest pleasure to give you both a ride, said Edwith.

Rachel said, "Ooh, thank you, Edwith, for the offer. If I can summon up the courage, I would appreciate it."

Paul smiled as he took her hand. "We can't be outdone by our son, can we?"

Everyone looked extremely surprised at Edwith's promise, and Jessynta praised his generosity.

Being Edwith, he said, *Perhaps that means I could try a little drop of something special . . . like your wine!*

"You really are such a cheeky dragon!" Paul laughed.

Jessynta tilted her head in Edwith's direction. *I must say, you have exceeded my expectations and been very well behaved, so you may have a small drop.*

Edwith bowed his head to her. *Thank you.*

Nat grinned at Pete.

Zara tilted her head in thought. "I wonder what my mother will think of all this when I tell her. Pete, tell me about your new portal. Is it fixed yet?"

"No, we have to do that when we get home, but we know what to do."

"Quite an eventful day again," remarked Paul, yawning widely and stretching his arms.

Jessynta noticed. *I think the adults should think about leaving. You have been here a little long.*

They began clearing up the picnic stuff.

You need not clear away the leftover food. I will clean it up, said Edwith, prompting roars of laughter from the humans. *Perhaps the other dragons can help me then.*

Pete heaved a big sigh, and his shoulders slumped. "Do you realize this could be the very last day we'll be using this portal? We will have to pack tomorrow."

Nat's jaw dropped. "Oh no, I hadn't realized. What if it won't work?" Tears formed in his eyes.

Edwith hopped close and stretched his wing out to cover him. *Nathaniel, do not look so miserable. I know you are scared. Do not worry. Jessynta can do everything she says she can. If she makes a single mistake, I will thump her with my tail and throw sand over her.* He lifted his tail, showering Nat with sand.

Laughing, Nat spat out a mouthful of sand, pushed him away, and brushed himself off.

"Edwith, you're so funny, and I do love you." Nat rubbed Edwith's muzzle until he purred. "Thank you. But perhaps if we pack most of our things tonight, we can try to squeeze in a quick visit."

"At the very least, we can do a video chat," said Pete. "I absolutely know the new portal is going to work just perfectly. I don't doubt your magic, Jessynta. Goodbye, see you outside our new portal as soon as we can." With tears in his eyes, he patted her scales.

Rayvinith lowered his head for Will.

"Goodbye for now, my feathered friend. See you soon." Will ruffled his feathers.

They all said goodbye to the Avalanyans. Pete looked at Zara. "In case we take a couple of days to get our portal up and running, please watch out for the dragons. If necessary, you can always video chat with us."

Paul and Rachel were rubbing their eyes as they thanked the Avalayans and followed the boys, who tearfully climbed the stairway to their portal.

When they passed through, Nat turned to take a good look at it. "You know what? I'll be quite sad not to see this old rock portal again."

"And I," said Pete.

"Me too," said Will.

When they were indoors again, their mother remarked, "I'm so impressed with Jessynta. How sensible and trustworthy she is. I'm so glad that she's in charge. I can't understand how easy I find it to trust her—a completely alien species."

Pete exchanged a knowing look with his brothers.

"I think when we get home, I'll have to shop for really glittery costume jewels for them all. " Rachel smiled at the thought.

Pete nodded. "You're probably right. Anyway, let's get a move on and see if we can do a little packing."

"Good idea," agreed their mother. "I think I'll take a nap before I start cooking dinner. After all the food we had there, I don't feel very hungry anyway."

The three boys dashed upstairs to make a start on packing.

"I'm sad," said Nat. "I really hope Jessynta's right and our new portal will work just as well, but I won't be able to relax until we get home and test it."

"She's extremely wise, and even if there is a problem, she'll work it out. I guess with magic, she can do anything, although I am inclined to agree with you both and won't be happy until we're home and all is sorted," said Pete.

"Come on everybody. Let's get a move on. The sooner we get this packing done, the more likely we are to find time for a quick chat tomorrow," said Will.

They rushed around like whirlwinds and managed to get everything packed except what they would need for the morning and the journey.

"You really have been hard at it, boys," said their mother when she saw all the slightly untidily packed bags and cases by the front door. "After I've cooked dinner, perhaps you can help me make a start on the kitchen." She tapped her forehead with a finger and gave a knowing smile. "I guess you've done all this so you have time left tomorrow to say goodbye to the dragons and the Avalanyans."

"Yes, what time will we be leaving?" asked Pete.

"We do want to make an early start, so as soon as we've eaten breakfast and washed the remaining dishes. Probably as close to nine as possible. The contract says we have to leave by ten anyway. You definitely won't have time to actually go there, but you have set up those tablets of ours so you can have virtual chats, haven't you? At least I think that's what you've been doing. Am I right?"

"We didn't think you understood all that scale stuff," said Pete.

"I don't pretend to get it all, but I do know the main bits. That dragon of yours is quite amazing. Anyway, the more you help tonight, the sooner we can get away tomorrow."

~~~~~

Pete shook Nat's arm. "Wake up, Nat. The sun is up, and it's nearly seven o'clock. I'm dressed. I'm going to wake Will."

A bleary-eyed Nat climbed out of bed. "No need to be so cheerful. I still wish we didn't have to go home."

"No worries. The sooner we get home, the sooner we can visit Avalanya again. Hurry up. After breakfast, we can call Jessynta."

The boys quickly got dressed and ran downstairs.

"Slow down, you must eat breakfast. We've a long journey ahead. I don't want to stop too often," said their father.

As soon as they finished, they excused themselves and tore off outside to get out the chairs for the last time. Casting a longing look up the hillside, Pete put the tablet on the chair and pressed Jessynta's icon, then waited patiently.

"Jessynta, we're nearly ready to leave. I'm pinning all our hopes on a successful portal installation," said Pete.

Brecchettya is here with Edwith and Rayvinith. I do not know where Crystalya and Zara are. I think they are searching the other side of the estuary with Zarven looking for more pretty shells and seaweed. Brecchettya, turn the camera so the boys can see Edwith and Rayvinith.

Good luck with your journey today. I would love to see those car machines you travel in. Though if I were there, I could fly you home a lot faster, said Edwith.
~~~~~

He is right, or maybe I could power your engine with my flames, suggested Rayvinith.

Will laughed. "Unfortunately, our machines don't use dragon fire."

A shout came from the cottage. "Boys, better put those chairs away and come back here. Dad's almost ready to go."

"Our mother's calling. It's time for us to go. It wasn't a long chat, but at least we managed a few minutes. Hope we can get our portal set up very soon." Pete closed up a little reluctantly. They put the chairs away.

As they drove away, Will said, "Bye, Lulworth Cove. Maybe we'll be back next year. Perhaps we could rent this cottage again. What a vacation it has been. London and school will be very tame after all this. What a pity we won't be able to share our adventures with our friends back there. Nobody would believe us."

#####

Be on the lookout for Christine Born's next book:

DRAGON MAGIC

CHARACTERS

EARTH PEOPLE
Living in London, England:
Peter (Pete) and Nathaniel (Nat): Fraternal twins, 12 years old
William (Will): Pete and Nat's brother, 10 years old
Rachel and Paul: Pete, Nat, and Will's parents

Recently moved to Virginia, USA:
Zara: the boys' first cousin, 11 years old
Anita (Rachel's sister) and Mark: Zara's parents

AVALANYANS
Living outside Estaria on a farm:
Brecchettya (pronounced Brek-ett-yah) (Brecky): 12 years old
Izchettya (pronounced Iz-kett-yah) (Izzy): 11 years old
Guillanya (pronounced Gwee-lan-yah) (Lanya): 10 years old
Skyla and Brin: Parents of Brecky, Izzy, and Lanya. Brin has gone missing.

Living in Estaria:
Zarven (Ven): the girls' cousin, 12 years old
Aleto (Brin's brother) and Suki (Skyla's sister): Ven's parents

DRAGONS

Jessynta (pronounced Jess-in-tah)
A turquoise blue, female, water dragon. As a water dragon, she mostly swims but flies by "swimming" the air currents using magic and frills on the side of her body.
Undisputed leader as the first dragon to hatch. She is a queen dragon, descended from a queen dragon who was the first to realize their world was threatened. Jessynta bonds with Pete and Brecky.

Edwith
A male, air dragon with scales. He is mostly green but in the light reflects colors of the rainbow. His powers are of the air. He bonds with Izzy and Nat.

Rayvinith (pronounced Ray-vin-ith)
A male, fire dragon who resembles a mythical South American Incan dragon with red feathers. He is able to breathe fire, although the thought frightens him. He bonds with Will and Lanya.

Crystalya (pronounced Cris-tal-yah)
A purple, female, earth dragon with sparkling jewels encrusting the spines of her wings. She has the ability to find minerals in the earth, make tunnels, and understand the flora and fauna. Animals and birds are often drawn to her and may talk to her. She bonds with Zara and Ven.

AUTHOR BIO

Christine Born was born in Surrey, south of London, England, at the start of World War II. She has vivid memories of air raids, middle-of-the-night races to bomb shelters, and the devastation to London as a result of bombing.

However, what lingers in her mind even more was the magical night when the war ended. To a child of six, that night was unbelievable. Until that day, there were no streetlights, and she often wondered what the poles in the streets were for. Now there were lights everywhere, and fireworks over the river.

That was the beginning of her love of magic and fantasy, and a hope for the end of wars. She became intrigued with the idea of other universes where dragons live and people cast magic spells. Because she loves working with children, she told and illustrated tales from ancient myths and fairy stories.

After attending art college then teacher college, Christine taught those with special needs, where her skills as a pianist and artist were put to good use.

Later she moved to the USA, married, and settled there. Life became very busy with three young children of her own, but Christine continued to teach and work with other children. She enjoyed composing short plays with song and dance and simplifying stories with illustrations for their enjoyment.

Throughout the years, she continued working with children, teaching Sunday school, running cub scout packs, working with playgroups, and instructing piano to beginners.

But she never lost her love of dragons. Inspired by her eldest three grandsons, she began to craft her first story. With the threat of pollution and climate change on her mind, she set the story in an alternate universe, where the human race has a chance to change their future.

Ancient Map of Avalanya

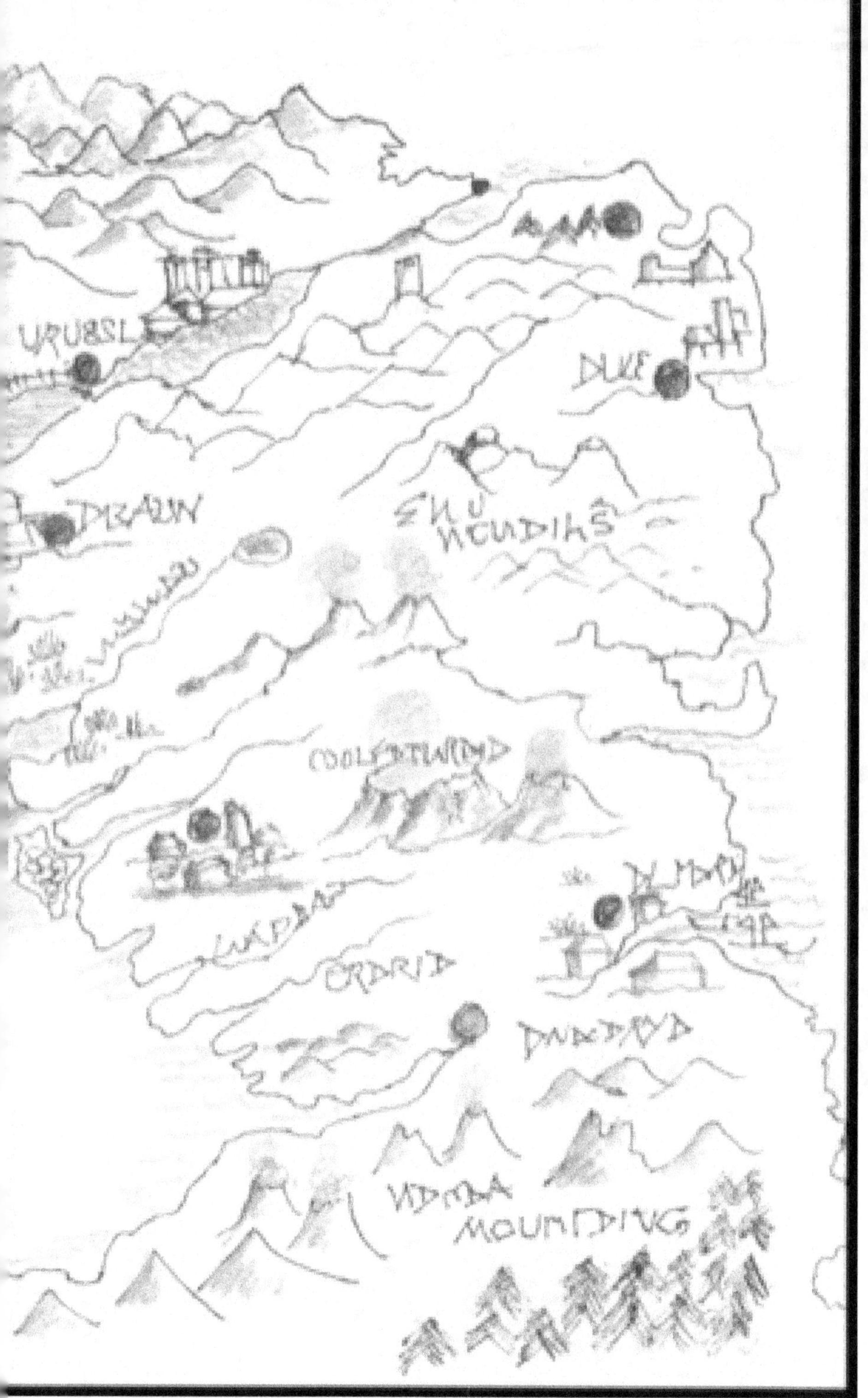
URUBSL
DUKE
DRARW
FNU MOUDIHS
COLENTIWRMD
URDAW
ORDRID
DARDAYD
VDMA MOUNTDING

www.ingramcontent.com/pod-product-compliance
Lightning Source LLC
Chambersburg PA
CBHW072123300726